Light Riders and the Fleur-de-lis Murder

Ann I. Goldfarb

To Lisa,
Hope you enjoy this adventure in time!
Fondly,
[illegible]
11/28/12

I enjoyed this book as well
Annie Brooks
2-21-24

Light Riders and the Fleur-de-lis Murder

Published by Ann I. Goldfarb
Time Travel Mysteries
Sun City West, Arizona, U.S.A.

ISBN 13: 978-1479271061
ISBN 10: 1479271063
Library of Congress Card Catalogue Number:
LCCN: 2012917187

This is a work of fiction. Names and characters are derived from the author's imagination. Any resemblance to people, living or deceased is purely coincidental. Historical locations are intended to give this work of fiction a sense of authenticity and reality. No parts of this book, with the exception of the study guide, may be reproduced without the author's consent. Visit the website:
www.timetravelmysteries.com

This book's interior and cover was designed by Jean Boles:
http://jeanboles.elance.com
Printed by CreateSpace

Light Riders and the Fleur-de-lis Murder

A Time Travel Mystery by
Ann I. Goldfarb

Also by this author:

THE FACE OUT OF TIME

RIPPLE RIDER: AN ANGUILLAN ADVENTURE IN TIME

THE LAST TAG

LIGHT RIDERS AND THE MORENCI MINE MURDER

In memory of my mother,
whose Bastille birthday and unusual
recollections of the French Revolution led me
to this time and place.

Prologue

"Aeden, wake-up! Wake-up! You were screaming in your sleep. Screaming in French!"

"I only know a few words, Ryn, mostly from restaurant menus. What did I say? *Omelette au fromage?"*

"You were speaking fluent French, Aeden, and it had nothing to do with food."

"So, what did I say?"

"Tirez la tête en arrière par les cheveux. Tranche lui la gorge d'un seul coup! Fais vite! Pull his head back by the hair and slit his throat with one move. Make it quick."

"Cut it out, Ryn. You must have been the one dreaming."

"I don't think so, Aeden. Everyone on the plane is looking at you. Good thing Mom and Dad are seated up front."

"Stop it, Ryn. You're scaring me."

PART ONE:

Another Dead Relative

Chapter One:
Aeden

The thud of Ryn's lacrosse stick as it hit its usual resting place in the kitchen corner jolted me momentarily. I could hear him yelling even though my room was at least twenty feet away. How could I concentrate on the five remaining algebra problems that were sitting in front of me with all that noise?

"What? Another dead relative? Another dead relative who's going to ruin spring break for me? This is so unfair! It was bad enough last summer when we had to clean out the hoarder's nest for great Auntie Zanne in Arizona. This stinks! This absolutely rots! I can't miss lacrosse practice. I just made varsity. This is unbelievable! Unbelievable and rotten. This..."

I could hear my brother getting louder and louder as he stormed out of the kitchen and down the hall to his room. Unfortunately, he was about to walk past mine. The door flew open without a knock and he stepped inside uninvited.

"How long have you known about this, Aeden?"

"I just found out a few minutes ago myself. And if you would have given Mom a chance to finish explaining, maybe you wouldn't be so furious," I replied.

"What's to explain? I'm going to miss lacrosse practice and have a lousy spring break. I'll be lucky if the coach even lets me onto the field when we get back. But what do you care?"

"Look, Ryn, I had plans, too; but you don't see me getting freaked out."

"That's because you're not on a team yet. Wait till you go out for something next year and then tell me how you feel about it."

"Doesn't matter. It's not going to change things. Mom and Dad already made the plane reservations. Besides, once you find out where we're going, you may actually like the idea."

"How can I like the fact that we're not going to be in Portland?"

"Because we're going to be in France. Paris, France to be exact. And you speak French, Ryn. You'll actually know what people are saying when we get there."

It was true. Ryn spoke fluent French. He took the language as an elective in 8th grade when he saw a yearbook picture of Mademoiselle Claudine and couldn't take his eyes off of her. I still remember that conversation at the dinner table. I thought my father was going to have a fit.

"What? You're selecting a language because you think the teacher is good looking? That's the most ridiculous thing I've ever heard. You choose to study something because it will benefit you in the future."

"This will benefit me. It will be one class that I won't fall asleep in!"

So Ryn studied French. And he really studied. I think he had the wildest crush on Mademoiselle Claudine and would do anything to please her. Including summer sessions and extra credit. So, it was no surprise that he became fairly fluent in less than three years. Not only that, but for some inexplicable reason, his name stopped becoming a permanent fixture on the detention list. My father couldn't argue with him anymore.

Ryn paused for a minute. Long enough to let it sink in.

"Paris? We're really going to Paris? I don't care who died. This is wonderful! *C'est merveilleux!*"

"Do you even listen to yourself? One minute you're all bent out of shape because you're going to miss lacrosse practice and the next minute you're ecstatic that someone in our family died."

"I'm not happy that some relative I didn't know died. I'm just happy they died in Paris. Paris! I've got to get on Mademoiselle Claudine's school website and tell her."

"You don't even know who it was!"

"OK, Aeden. So tell me. Who died? Which one of our long lost relatives died?"

"Great, great, great Uncle Henri. The youngest brother of Mom's great grandfather. And he didn't just die."

"What do you mean he didn't just die?"

"He didn't just die, Ryn, because he was murdered."

Chapter Two:
Aeden

"Murdered? This great, great, whatever uncle of ours that we never knew was murdered? How can they be sure? I mean the guy must've been ancient. Maybe he just died of old age."

"No, he was murdered all right, Ryn. A knife to his throat. That's why we're all going to Paris. Mom's been on the phone long distance with the investigators all morning. It wasn't an ordinary murder. At least that's what she said. The police want to talk with the family so we've got no choice but to go to France."

"What are we going to tell the police? We didn't even know this great, great uncle."

"We didn't, but maybe Mom and Dad did. There's a lot of stuff we don't know about family members."

"Well, I know one thing. I'm emailing Mademoiselle Claudine right now. No, better yet, I'm heading back to the school. It'll only take me a few minutes on my bike and she's bound to be there. She always stays late working in her classroom."

"You'd better be back in time for dinner or Mom will really be pissed."

Ryn shrugged off my warning and charged into the garage for his bike, but not before barking a command at me.

"Tell Mom I had to go back to school for something."

"What?"

"I don't care, Aeden. Just tell her I forgot something. Geez, you always make such a big deal out of everything!"

I could hear the garage door cranking up and down. My mom heard it, too, but by the time she looked outside, Ryn was halfway down the block on his bike. I heard her grumble just as she knocked on my door.

"Guess your brother is furious with us for ruining his spring break. You'd think we did it on purpose. So, where's he off to? Just blowing off steam?"

"I don't know, Mom. He said he forgot something at school. He'll be back for dinner. Ryn's stomach has more sense than he does.

But I told him about the murder and the fact that we were going to France. I don't think he's going to be all that upset about missing lacrosse."

"About your great, great Uncle Henri...No one knows about the murder. And no one needs to know. Just be sure that you and your brother don't say anything about it to anyone until we find out the circumstances. If anyone asks, just tell them we have an incredible opportunity to visit Paris. Not exactly a lie...but we need to be circumspect about Uncle Henri's death. Do you understand?"

I nodded before speaking.

"I'm sure Ryn will understand, too."

"Good. I've got tons of things to do before dinner so just finish up your homework. We'll talk later."

I could feel my stomach twisting and turning as my mom closed the door. By now Ryn was sure to have told Mademoiselle Claudine about the murder. But he really didn't have much more information. I only hoped he didn't decide to make a quick stop at the computer room and post it on Facebook. That would be just like Ryn. Anything for attention. And my mother would be furious. No one was to know. Especially his French teacher.

The minute the door was closed, I sent Ryn a quick text and hoped I wasn't too late. Then I tried to concentrate on my homework, but all I could think about was the murder and the fact that we would be in Paris by the end of the week.

When I heard someone coming in through the garage I immediately raced to the kitchen door.

"Ryn? Is that you?"

"Sorry to disappoint you, Aeden, it's just your dad. And why are you in such a hurry to see Ryn? You two usually avoid each other."

"It's that obvious, huh?"

"Seems that way lately, but maybe a week in Paris will change things for both of you. I'm sure Mom has shared the news by now."

"Yeah, she did. So when do we leave?"

"Day after tomorrow. As soon as school is out. We were lucky to get a direct flight but there was no way we could all sit together. You'll be stuck with your brother."

"That's OK. I'm used to him."

"What do mean 'use to me?' You make it sound like some condition or affliction that someone has to get used to. Like a disease."

I turned my head to the doorway.

"How long have you been standing there, Ryn?"

"I just walked in. I had to tell my coach that I would be missing practice."

"Mademoiselle Claudine is coaching lacrosse these days?"

Ryn shot me a dirty look and started for his room, pausing briefly to catch what our father was saying.

"Both of you had better make an effort to get along. If nothing else, do it for your mother's sake. This can't be easy for her."

"What do you mean?" I said. "We weren't even close to this great, great uncle."

"Close enough, apparently. Your mother was the only one named in his will."

Ryn shrugged as he edged further away from the room.

"What's so odd about that? People are named in wills all the time."

My father's words were slow and deliberate.

"Because the will was written long before she was even born."

Chapter Three:
Ryn

I couldn't believe how bossy, snippy and annoying Aeden had become. *What did you tell Mademoiselle Claudine about the trip? Did you say anything at all about the murder? Because you weren't supposed to open your mouth. What do your friends know? I didn't say anything to my friends even though I was tempted. I know how to keep* ***my*** *mouth shut.*

The thought of sitting next to her on a plane for the next 13 hours was enough to drive anyone insane. But I had no choice. It was a late booking and my parents had seats up front. Aeden and I were crammed in the middle of the plane with two or three people on either side of us. Crammed and cramped were the key words.

Aeden had just gotten an eReader for her birthday so I figured she'd leave me alone. I figured wrong.

"Oh my gosh, Ryn. When did you get an iPad2? Did you download any movies? Let me see it."

"Keep your hands off, Aeden. I borrowed it from the computer library at school. If anything happens to it, Mom and Dad will go ballistic."

"Fine. I'm not interested anyway."

She took out her eReader and pretended not to notice. Unfortunately, the other passengers did, beginning with the middle-aged guy who was seated next to me.

"Are you traveling alone with your sister?"

"No, our parents are just a few seats away."

"That's good to know. Traveling abroad can be so... well, let's just say one needs to be careful these days."

"Uh-huh," I replied, looking around to see if anyone else was listening. The woman, who was apparently traveling with him, gave him a nudge.

"You're going to scare that boy. Getting on a plane is frightening enough, what with terrorists, birds flying into the engines, computer malfunctions, why it's a miracle at all we can land in one piece!"

I leaned over to get a better look at her face.

"Now who's scaring him, Julia? Never mind, everything will be just fine."

"Sure," I replied. "Just fine."

I could think of lots of words to describe the next 13 hours and believe me, the word "fine" wasn't one of them. Aeden barely spoke and every time I got up to use the restroom, the other passengers acted as if the imposition would kill them. Our parents came back two or three times to make sure we were OK, each time telling us that they would be waiting by the exit the minute the plane landed.

It was a direct flight but not a non-stop. Still, we wouldn't be landing in Amsterdam until the next morning. And then on to Paris. I was wedged into my seat so tight that my butt couldn't even sweat. Even the iPad2 didn't take my mind off the fact that I was getting more and more uncomfortable by the minute. I glanced at Aeden from time to time. If she was uncomfortable, she never let on, just to piss me off.

The on-board entertainment was some boring movie about a woman who was divorcing her husband and starting a business growing lavender. I wanted to poke my eyes out with a fork! Dinner was minuscule—stuffed chicken the size of a McNugget, a spoonful of mashed potatoes, peas and some sort of pastry. At least they had soda.

Aeden ate without saying a word. Typical Aeden. Whenever she gets angry, she just gives you the cold shoulder. Still, it was better than her nagging.

Then the flight attendants determined that it was time for everyone to sleep. Even those of us who were wide awake. They closed the window blinds and dimmed the lights. Distributed blankets and pillows for anyone who wanted them. I watched as my sister propped the small pillow behind her head and closed her eyes.

The plane had gotten still in the fake nighttime. I decided to check out a few websites while everyone slept and that's when Aeden went berserk.

Chapter Four:

Ryn

"Holy crap, Aeden. You woke the whole plane up screaming like that!"

Even in the dim light, I could tell by the look on my sister's face that she had no idea what I was talking about. And when I tried to explain, she got downright hostile.

"Stop making stuff up, Ryn. I must have had a nightmare, that's all."

Then, the twenty-something guy with the dark glasses who was sitting next to her, and who was oblivious to us up until now, suddenly decided to speak. In French, no less.

"Vous hurlaient tous les droits, et vous sembliez savoir beaucoup sur égorger des gens. Ll suffit de ne pas le mien coupé."

"He said you were screaming all right and that you seemed to know a lot about cutting people's throats," I said, as Aeden gave the guy a strange look. "And he said not to cut his."

Aeden flinched as if I had just hurled the worst insult at her.

"How do I know that's what he really said, Ryn?"

"Your brother understands French quite well," the guy responded. "And no doubt so do you."

"I don't speak French. Honestly. Just a few words. Mostly from menus. I don't..."

The guy smiled, put on a headset and turned his attention to his laptop, as if none of this had happened.

"That was really creepy, Ryn. Really creepy."

"So you're talking to me now?"

"Yeah, guess so. But I don't understand. How could I have spoken fluent French?"

"Maybe it was a line from some old movie you once saw, or..."

"Or what?"

"Maybe you did speak French at one time."

"You're not saying..."

"What? That you went back in time? We did it once before."

"That was almost two years ago and nothing's happened since."

"Well, maybe something will. I mean, think about it. The police obviously can't solve Uncle Henri's murder. That's why they want to speak with Mom and Dad. So, just suppose you and I were able to go back in time, just before he gets killed."

"And do what? Stop him from getting murdered?"

"Can't do that, Aeden. No one can alter the events that already took place. But, we can find out who did it."

"We could get ourselves killed in the process. And besides, we don't know if we can really go back. And what if we don't return this time?"

"You're sitting here. In the now. That means we already returned."

"Even if we could go back, Ryn. I don't want to take the risk. It was awful last time."

"Awful? All you had to do was wash a few pots and pans. I was glued to a horse for days on end thinking each minute was going to be my last. I mean, those men had guns and liked using them. I should be the one refusing to take a chance."

"You just want to solve Uncle Henri's murder to impress Mademoiselle Claudine."

"That thought never crossed my mind. But now that you mention it, I have even more reason to find a way back."

"Good luck with that, Ryn. Because I'm not going."

"Too late. From what you were screaming, you were already there. Might as well go back to sleep. They'll be waking us up with a microscopic breakfast in no time."

Aeden fluffed her pillow, placed it behind her head and closed her eyes. I was about to do the same when I caught a glimpse of the computer guy turning his head slowly to get a good look at my sister's face. He caught my eye and whispered.

"Gorges de certaines personnes méritent d'être coupé, vous le savez. Some people's throats deserve to be cut, you know."

I didn't say anything. I just leaned back, shut my eyes and dozed off until morning. When the captain announced that we were 90 minutes from Amsterdam, the guy sitting next to Aeden was gone. I figured he was either in the restroom or perhaps visiting with another passenger. The odd thing was that we never saw him again. I kept telling myself that it was nothing unusual. I mean, these jumbo planes hold hundreds of passengers and ours was no exception. Still, we didn't see him during our brief stop at the Amsterdam terminal, and when we re-boarded the plane, a young couple from Italy was seated next to my sister and for some reason, it really freaked her out.

"What happened to the other guy? The one with the dark glasses?"

"How am I supposed to know, Aeden? He didn't share his itinerary with me."

"Well, what did he say? He whispered something to you."

"It wasn't important."

"If it wasn't important, then just tell me."

I didn't want to make Aeden any more nervous and jerky than she already was, so I told her that he just said "have a good trip."

"All those words for 'have a good trip'?"

"Yeah, Aeden, what can I say? It's a complicated language."

She gave me one of her "I don't believe you" looks and I wondered if she had understood what the guy really said. And if she did, then how was that possible?

Chapter Five: Aeden

"Ryn, Aeden! Stay together! Your father's got the passports and we need to move quickly through customs."

My mother ushered us along the corridor that led from the plane to the baggage area. Up ahead, my father was already standing in front of one of the large carousels, waiting for it to spit out our bags. I was still groggy from the plane ride and my head felt too heavy to process anything. Ryn, on the other hand, was his usual whining self.

"Was that supposed to be a croissant we had for breakfast? Because if it was, then it was terrible—all mushy like someone nuked it too long in the microwave."

"I didn't even eat my breakfast, Ryn. I was still asleep when they served it. What time is it anyway?"

"It's morning in Paris. I don't know. I didn't turn my watch ahead."

"It's 7:45 a.m. Parisian time," my mother said as she continued to herd us down the hall. "Stop grumbling and hurry up. Once we get through customs, a police officer will be escorting us directly to a station in the 7th arrondissement where Uncle Henri lived. Apparently, the 7th is quite a wealthy neighborhood. Your great uncle owned the apartment. That's where he was found..."

"We know," Ryn said before my mother could continue. "Dead. Killed. Knife to the throat. What? What are you two looking at?"

The corridor had gotten quiet and Ryn's voice boomed out like an announcement. I stopped walking long enough to respond.

"Everyone's listening, Ryn and they probably understand English."

I knew I was right. People looked at the three of us as if we were terrorists.

"Hope you're happy, Ryn. We'll probably be placed on the 'No-Fly' list."

"I'll just give them your name, Aeden."

"Enough with the both of you," my mother grumbled. "Your father's got the bags, now get a move on!"

"Will we be staying at Uncle Henri's apartment?" I asked.

"No, honey. It's still a crime scene. We've got reservations at a hotel that's a few blocks away. Check-in time is 3:00 p.m. so it looks as if we'll be spending most of the morning at the police station."

If Ryn's voice was loud before, it practically boomed this time.

"What? I have to stay in these sweaty wrinkled clothes for another day? I need to take a shower or something."

"Well, I need to brush my teeth, Ryn. You don't see me complaining about it."

"You could have done that on the plane, Aeden. It's not my fault you don't think of things."

Before I could say another word, we had reached the customs line and everything got deadly still. Even Ryn knew when to keep his mouth shut.

"VIDEZ VOS POCHES S'IL VOUS PLAÎT!" came a voice from behind a counter.

"VIDEZ VOS POCHES S'IL VOUS PLAÎT! EMPTY YOUR POCKETS PLEASE!"

The only thing in my pockets was a stick of gum. My house keys, cell phone and purse were already being scanned. I reached for the gum but it wasn't there. Maybe I had chewed it and forgotten. Then I felt the paper. The paper, but not the gum. I pulled it out to show the agent but it wasn't a gum wrapper. It was a small piece of paper with a note. One I hadn't written. One I couldn't have possibly written because it was in French.

"Very funny, Ryn," I said as I waved the note in front of his face. "Did you put this in my pocket?"

Ryn shook his head and grabbed the paper. "You said you found this in your pocket? I don't understand."

"What do you mean?"

"It's a note, Aeden. But the handwriting looks as if it's from another century. All fancy cursive in dark ink."

The agent glanced at the piece of paper and motioned for us to keep on going in the line.

"Maybe that guy on the plane put it in my pocket," I whispered to Ryn as we grabbed our bags and followed our parents to an open area just beyond the security section. "What does it say?"

N'hésitez pas la prochaine fois ou il sera votre sang sur le bout de la lame.

"In English, Ryn. What does it say in English?"

"Just a stupid note. Forget it. It was probably meant for someone else. Now come on, Mom and Dad are waiting."

Ryn shoved the paper into his jeans and poked my elbow to get moving.

Looking straight ahead at the large double-glass doors, I could see taxicabs lined up on one side of the street and limousines on the other. There were people holding signs in a roped off area to our left. Signs for passengers.

"There's our contact," shouted my father. "Come on, he'll take us to the car."

Minutes later, we were seated in the back of a limousine and headed toward a police station. The ride took about 40 minutes—fast highways, then large city streets. Too bad I was so drowsy that I didn't even notice the Eiffel Tower.

Maybe it was jet lag or lack of sleep but I felt as if I was disconnected from my own body. Even when we were ushered into a large conference room at the police station and offered breakfast rolls and coffee, all I really wanted to do was sleep. The room could have been anywhere. Nothing indicated that we were even in France except for a small sign on the door that read "Sortie."

Ryn was still muttering about needing to change his clothes when a heavy-set officer sat down next to us and began to speak. I was relieved it was in English. At last I'd know what was going on.

"Thank you all for your cooperation in this matter. We appreciate your willingness to meet directly with us regarding the death of your uncle, Monsieur Henri Chastain. This is a sensitive matter, therefore we could not reveal anything more than cursory information to you over the phone."

I could see through my mother's composure and knew that beneath her slight smile, she was tense and worried. My father gave her hand a slight squeeze as the officer continued speaking.

"You were told that your uncle was stabbed in his apartment, a knife to his throat. That, I am afraid is not exactly the truth."

"You mean he wasn't stabbed?" Ryn blurted out as he tried to straighten the wrinkles from his shirt.

"Stabbed is not the correct word. I am not sure of the English word. In French, *sabrer*."

"Slit open. Slashed." Ryn said. Then he shifted immediately to French.

"Quelqu'un a réduit sa gorge. Someone slashed his throat."

"Oui. Quelqu'un a réduit sa gorge," the officer continued. "But not an ordinary cut to

throat. A slash, as you say, but with a final cut at the end."

My mother looked horrified.

"What do you mean?"

"Whoever killed your uncle left a message. A small cut in the shape of a fleur-de-lis was at the bottom of his neck."

"Were there more murders of this type?" my father asked as he locked eyes with the officer.

"Yes, many more."

Then Ryn yelled out, "We're talking serial killer! No wonder they wanted us here."

"I believe I answered too soon," the officer replied. "Yes, there were many killings with the throat slashed and the fleur-de-lis cut deep into the skin. But not in this century. France has not seen a murder like this since the 1700s, at the height of *La Revolution*. There was even a name for it, *fleur-de-lis assassiner.*"

"Fleur-de-lis murder?" Ryn continued. "Maybe it was just some nut case."

The officer nodded and then shrugged as if he had second thoughts.

"There is always that possibility, but we have reason to believe it goes beyond a single assassin."

My voice was soft but I managed to ask, "What makes you say that?"

The officer opened a small attaché case and took out a piece of paper that seemed to be obscured with blood stains.

"Because, mademoiselle, a note was found next to the body and it was written in plural. See for yourself."

He set the paper directly in front of us and Ryn read it out loud.

"NOUS AVONS MAINTENANT LA JUSTICE."

"WE NOW HAVE JUSTICE."

I felt clammy and lightheaded all at once.

"I think I need a glass of water."

The officer must have seen the color leave my face.

"Forgive me; this has to be very difficult for all of you. Our driver will take your family to the hotel. I will contact you later today. We need to meet at your uncle's apartment. There may be clues we are unaware of. Family matters. Things only you will recognize and understand."

My mother's eyes darted from the note to the officer.

"But we never knew our uncle."

"Perhaps, but you most certainly knew his brother, your great grandfather."

Chapter Six: Aeden

I was irritable and exhausted. To make matters worse, Ryn didn't stop complaining.

"Do I have to share a room with Aeden? I better not have to share a room with Aeden!"

"Keep it down, Ryn," my father muttered as the driver took us to the hotel. "We have a family suite. You and your sister will have your own rooms. Once we get there, you should get washed and changed. We'll grab a bite to eat before the police return to take us to your uncle's apartment."

We've stayed at hotel chains before in Phoenix and Tucson, but none of them looked as extravagant and elegant as the one in Paris. Uncle Henri must have been swimming in money to live in a neighborhood like this. I started to unpack my bag when Ryn cracked the door open and motioned for me.

"Aeden, listen. I meant what I said on the plane. I really think we can use refracted light to go back in time and see exactly what happened to our great, great uncle. I've worked on those old formulas and I know what went wrong the last time."

"Everything went wrong, Ryn. Everything! We got separated for one thing. How can you be sure that won't happen again?"

"Last time you stood in front of me. Even that slight vertical distance made a difference. This time you'll be right next to me."

"There won't be a *this time* because I refuse to do it!"

"Stop being so obstinate. Don't you realize that if the police can't solve Uncle Henri's murder then Mom and Dad are going to get stuck with all sorts of paperwork and legalities? Heck, they won't be able to sell his apartment or any of his possessions. It'll be a mess that drags on for years."

I had to admit, my brother was right. Still, it was a dangerous plan. And I wasn't sure he had really thought it out. So I asked.

"And how are we going to do this again? This time travel thing. You didn't pack any of the old prisms and that's the only way I know we can move through time."

"Didn't have to, Aeden," Ryn responded with a grin. "We're just a few subway stops away from the largest prism of all—the pyramid in front of the Louvre. It's all reflective glass. Just need a small pocket mirror and I think we can do this."

"But Mom and Dad won't let us out of their sight."

"That's what you think. Just watch."

Next thing I knew, Ryn was in our parents' room insisting that he and I visit the Louvre while Mom and Dad are stuck with the police. Insisting and whining.

"I can't miss an opportunity like this. What am I supposed to tell people? What am I supposed to tell Mademoiselle Claudine? That I spent an entire week in Paris and the only thing I saw was my dead uncle's apartment and the police station?"

I could hear my mother's voice rising above Ryn's moans.

"He does have a point, you know."

Then my father responded.

"They're still awfully young to be left on their own in the city."

"They'll just be at the museum. We'll have a driver drop them off tomorrow morning and we can pick them up later in the day when we're finished with the police business. And

Ryn does speak the language after all. They'll be fine."

"All right," my father said. "You and your sister can spend the day at the Louvre. Can't very well say you've visited Paris without seeing the Mona Lisa."

"That's terrific! Aeden and I will be okay. Nothing to worry about!"

"Good. Now finish un-packing and get washed. And don't spend all day in the shower. The rest of us want to go out to eat. Get a move on!"

Ryn mouthed two words at me as he headed to the bathroom.

"Told you."

I shrugged my shoulders at him and looked at my clothes.

"Ryn," I whispered. "The clothes. What if they're all wrong?"

"Don't be ridiculous. We're only slipping back a few days. Fashions don't change in a few days. Jeans and t-shirts are fine."

"But what if..."

"Stop worrying. You're worse than Mom."

Then he trailed off to the bathroom, closing the door with a loud thud.

I knew Ryn had spent time with the old formula, because that's the kind of thing he enjoys. He'd make a great physicist someday.

But as I held up my only other pair of jeans I had the strangest sensation that everything was wrong. A feeling. A glimpse. I don't know. But something told me that jeans were not the thing I should have been wearing. I only wish I had listened.

Chapter Seven:
Ryn

Why Aeden ordered the fish stew is beyond me. I kept telling her that she'd hate it and she did. But did she listen to me? Of course not. Then she wanted to eat half of my coq au vin. At least I knew one thing about food. You can't go wrong with chicken.

The restaurant was just across the street from our hotel, but thanks to a drizzling rain, we were all damp by the time we walked there. None of us thought to bring jackets or even a sweatshirt.

My parents kept looking at their cell phones, waiting for a call from the police. And sure enough, about the time our dessert was being served, the call came in. We had exactly ten minutes before someone was going to take us to Uncle Henri's apartment, or "the scene of the crime" as they put it.

Another black limousine and a quick ride to the most imposing building on the street. It was brick, five stories high with wrought iron balconies and fancy doorways. It was also old. Older than Napoleon himself. Uncle Henri's apartment was the entire fourth floor, complete with his own private elevator. Last serviced by Napoleon, too, I'm sure, so I took the stairs instead. Good thing, because the elevator only held three people at a time.

Two police officers were standing guard by the door when I arrived; and even though I'm in pretty good shape, I was still panting when I got there. The others were already inside. Finally, a chance to use my French.

"Ma famille est en attente pour moi à l'intérieur."

"Yes," responded one of the officers in perfect English. "Your family is waiting for you inside so please go right in."

I turned the ornate bronze doorknob and stepped inside. Uncle Henri was rich all right. The place reeked of money. Large mahogany and leather furniture, fancy oriental rugs, bronze statues, hand carved stones in showcases, and a table that was really a large compass. Oil paintings of hunting scenes and animals seemed to be everywhere. And everything was absolutely neat. Dust would be too intimidated to settle here. I stood in front of a large bronze egret and tried to sort things out. What was Uncle Henri like? If his apartment was any indication, then I'd say formal, demanding and particular.

Aeden was glued to a small showcase that housed tiny figurines. She turned her head my way for just a second before speaking.

"Mom and Dad are in the master bedroom with the police. That's where Uncle Henri was found. They don't want us to go in there."

"Good grief. It's not as if the body's still there," I said as I made my way to the door. "It isn't still there, is it?"

"Don't Ryn! I mean it! They said not to go in."

"So what are we supposed to do? Stand around the living room looking at his stuff?"

"Something may give us a clue to his death."

"Yeah, his collection of porcelain."

I walked through the living room and into the kitchen. Uncle Henri must've had it remodeled recently because everything looked new. Granite countertops. Stainless steel appliances. A large overhead contraption that held all sorts of pots and pans. And three different coffee machines. But it was the smell that filled my nostrils the minute I walked in. Not an awful stench like a dead body or rotting food, but a fruity, lemony, orangey smell that seemed to be older than time. I tried to place it and then I saw the small nook behind the refrigerator. Uncle Henri was leaving at least five or six grapefruits out to ripen. Well, they ripened all right. They were wrinkled, withered and reeking citrus. *Someone will have lots of fun cleaning out this kitchen and it better not be me.*

"Ryn, what are you doing?"

I could hear my father's voice clear across the room.

"Just checking out the kitchen."

"Stay in the living room and for heaven's sake, don't touch anything."

I wandered back in and Aeden was still looking at those figurines.

"What do you suppose these are, Ryn? They look like tiny boxes with hinges."

"They're Limoges and for heaven's sakes, put that one down! We learned about them in French class. The originals were snuffboxes made in the 1700s for the aristocracy. If they're real, they must be worth a fortune."

"They're adorable! Little dogs. Cats. Birds. Small baskets with wine and cheese, and look, here's one with an odd Fleur-de-lis on top, the same design as..."

Then Aeden got still and turned away from the showcase.

"We'll figure it out, Aeden," I whispered. "We'll get back here before any other Fleurs-de-lis wind up on people's necks."

"Are you sure?"

"Pretty sure. The worst thing that can happen is that we'll get back a few weeks before the murder instead of a few days. Then we'll just have to wait it out. But time will catch up with us. It always does."

But I was wrong. The laws of refraction were apparently meant to be broken. I just wish I had known.

Chapter Eight:
Ryn

I could feel the crumpled note in my pocket as I slipped out of my jeans and into an old pair of sweats. It was a relief that Aeden didn't press me for more information. I mean, after all, who wants to get a note that says not to hesitate or "it will be your blood on the tip of the blade." Certainly not my sister. She'd freak.

My parents had arranged for a hotel driver to take us to the Louvre shortly after breakfast. But everything would depend on the weather. If the murky grey sky and drizzle continued, there'd be no way the sun would bounce off the prisms that Aeden's compact mirror would create from the glass triangles in the Louvre Pyramid. And no way to move through time. I just hoped the weather would clear up before morning as I pulled the duvet over my head and closed my eyes. I needed a good night's sleep if I was going to be clear-headed tomorrow.

"The sun better be up," I muttered to myself as I opened my eyes. "If it's raining, I'll be forced to spend the entire day with Aeden as she swoons over the Impressionists. What is it about girls and Impressionist paintings? It better not be raining. And besides, we really need to do this."

But it wasn't sunshine. It was Aeden, flicking the light on next to my bed just as soon as I had dozed off.

"Ryn, I couldn't sleep. I'm really scared about this. Something doesn't feel right."

"Yeah, it's called sleep deprivation. Honestly Aeden, go back to bed. We'll be all right. Just be sure to take your compact mirror with you. Leave everything else at the hotel. Okay?"

"I guess so. You're sure you've calculated this right?"

"I did. I'll know just where to stand when we get there, depending upon the exact hour of the day. But one thing for sure. We've got to be at least five feet away from anyone or they'll wind up with us."

"How are we going to manage that? The Louvre is always crowded."

"There are lulls. Just stay with me and quit worrying so much."

"Fine. Night Ryn, see you in the morning. Oh, I almost forgot. I need to tell you something about that figurine in Uncle Henri's apartment."

"Now? Now you want to talk about Limoges? Go to sleep, Aeden. It can wait."

Aeden closed the door and I shut off the light. But it wasn't as easy getting back to sleep. I kept thinking about that note and Uncle Henri's murder. Could we have had something to do with it in another time? The thought rattled me and I reached for another blanket.

Darkness. Quiet. And then an alarm.

"Bonjour. Il est 7 heures du matin."

The morning wake-up call. It was 7:00 a.m. I could make out faint sunshine through the curtains and got up to take a closer look. We were in luck. The drizzly rain was gone. The suite had two bathrooms and I rushed to beat Aeden. She was still asleep when I got out of the shower.

"Wake up, Aeden," I shouted as I cracked open the door to her room. "Don't want to miss our exciting day at the Louvre."

The minutes seemed to drag as our folks droned on and on about staying together even if it was a gallery that we didn't enjoy. I just nodded and continued to eat the fruits and pastries that were on my plate, ignoring the strange looking yogurt.

Then a quick double ring on the phone.

"Must mean your driver's ready," my mom said. "Have a good time. We'll meet you back at the hotel this afternoon. Then dinner."

"Sounds great, Mom," I said.

Then my dad spoke.

"Remember what your mother said. Stay together. Keep an eye on your sister."

"I can take care of myself," Aeden quipped.

"Yeah," I said, "but you won't get too far with your limited vocabulary that consists mainly of cheese products."

Before she could say another word, I tossed her the hoodie that was on the couch and grabbed mine.

"We'll be fine," I shouted as we headed to the elevator but not before Aeden kicked my ankle.

"Cheese products?"

"Yeah, cheese products, and apparently throat cutting. At least in your sleep."

Chapter Nine: Aeden

The crowd in front of the Louvre seemed endless. Kids with parents, couples holding hands, students and teachers, groups of women, a few men in business suits, and of course, screaming babies.

Ryn was already familiar with the set-up and he motioned me toward a side of the pyramid that faced what looked like some sort of shallow swimming pool.

"The main entrance is over there. See the sign. It will take visitors down an escalator to the main floor. We need to be on the other side. Follow me."

The sun created ripples on the surface of the pool, each one reflected in the pyramid's tiny triangles. I watched as Ryn walked near the structure, his eyes fixed on the edge closest to the old part of the museum.

"No one's near us, Aeden, so listen carefully. Take your mirror, but keep your other hand over it for the time being and point it directly at this triangle. Keep it at arm's length. As soon as I get to your side, uncover it and grab my hand. Got it?"

"You're sure we're going to be okay?"

"Positive. Now do as I say. Quickly, before anyone walks around the corner of the pyramid."

The small mirror was shaking in my hand and I tried to steady it. What if my shaking causes it to do something different? I didn't even want to consider those possibilities. I took a slow, deep breath and waited for Ryn. *Grab his hand. That's all I have to do. Just grab his hand as soon as he steps over here.*

Everything seemed to happen in slow motion. At first it was barely audible, but then the shrieks and giggling got louder. It was a baby. A toddler. Some kid was running from his mother or his babysitter or who-knows-who, but he ran right into us. His shrieks of laughter stung my ears like little wasps.

"Vous ne pouvez pas me rattraper, Maman! Vous ne pouvez me rattraper!"

Maman. Mother. It was a kid's game. Like "Catch me if you can." He was just a few feet from his mother's arms but a few feet would be hours or even days in the past. I tried to cover the mirror but the light hit it too fast. Blinding. Searing. Burning. I felt something tighten on my wrist as I tried to stop my knees from shaking. Ryn's hand. Ryn was grabbing me. But what about the kid? The toddler. This was the worst scenario I could imagine. What if that child...? I tried to force the thought out of my mind.

My body felt as if it were trapped inside a coil—paralyzed, suffocating. And the light was so intense that I didn't dare open my eyes. I could feel Ryn's hand closing tighter on my wrist. *You better not let go of me, Ryn. Not for a second.* Some sort of movement and the light changed. Bouncing off the tip of my eyelids, alternating from light to dark. Energy. The energy of time itself, before matter. The coil was unyielding, but Ryn's hand remained clasped to my wrist. I had to force myself to breathe. It wasn't coming naturally. *Hang on to me, Ryn.* Light and dark waves continued to pulsate across my face. But something was different. The light got shorter. More dark waves until finally the light was gone all together. Only darkness. I tried to open my eyes but they were too heavy. I could feel Ryn's fingers slowly slipping away from my wrist. *No. Don't you let go! Don't you dare let go of me.*

The vise that held me started to loosen. I'd be free. Free to look around and find Ryn. I could open my eyes if I tried. I could...if it weren't for the ringing in my ears. An awful, high pitched ringing that made me dizzy and weak all at once. It was slow, this strange feeling. The movement from an upright position to the floor. Is this what fainting feels like? And the toddler? Was he fainting too?

You shouldn't have let go of me, Ryn. You shouldn't have let go.

Chapter Ten:
Ryn

Honestly. That kid should have been tethered to his mother with a leash or something if she couldn't control him. Yeah, yeah, he was just a baby, but thanks to him, Aeden and I got shoved out of range. One slip and I had no idea where the light would take us on the time-space continuum. The only thing I saw before the nausea and spinning orbs took over was the mother pulling the kid away from us. A quick blink and they were unscathed. As for my sister and me, well... it was a nightmare.

I held on to Aeden's wrist as long as I could, but something was forcing me to the ground and I couldn't control it. To make matters worse, I couldn't seem to open my eyes for the longest time, and when I did, everything was dark. Only snippets of light appeared in the distance. My mind felt strangely disconnected from my body. I could hear the sound of water running through pipes and then, I felt it. Water. Crap! My clothing was all wet. And it smelled of something. Musty. Dirty. An old stench of rotten leaves. Where the heck were we?

Aeden's scream echoed through the darkness, making it impossible for me to find her.

"Stop screaming, Aeden. I'm right here. Your screams just echo. Talk softly. Can you follow my voice?"

"I can hear you Ryn, but I can't move. It's too slippery. I'll fall. And the wall is wet, too. I'm pressed against it. Ryn, there's water below, running water. And that kid, that baby, what if..."

"The kid's fine, Aeden. We just got flipped forward. In that last flash of light I saw his mother grabbing him. He's safe. Stay where you are; I'll get closer."

My eyes were getting accustomed to the semi-darkness but there was no getting use to the odor.

"Hang on, Aeden. We're just in some sort of tunnel."

"It's a sewer, Ryn. We're in a sewer. Under the streets of Paris. Even I could figure that one out and I don't speak French!"

"A sewer! A SEWER! My clothes are going to reek. My sneaks will be ruined. These sewers could go for miles under the street. All because of that jerky little kid!"

"Quit complaining and come get me. I feel as if I'm about to slip. Hurry up!"

"Just stay where you are. I'll get to you."

Unbelievable. Of all the rotten lousy places we could find ourselves in, it had to be a sewer. It was bad enough that I was stepping in who-knows-what as I made my way to Aeden on a narrow stone walkway. Good thing the place was dark. I didn't want to know what was there. Smelling it was bad enough. And the walls were wet. At least that's what Aeden said. I wasn't about to reach over and see for myself. In fact, I kept a fair distance from the wall. No way was I going to have my clothes rub against centuries of rot and debris. I inched my way slowly to the sound of her voice.

"Come on, Ryn. I mean it. I'm slipping and there's water down here. Lots of water."

Just then, I heard the sound of Aeden's scream. Sharp and loud. Then cut off in mid-breath.

"Aeden, are you..."

But it was another voice that responded. A male voice.

"Tais-toi! Les soldats du roi."

It was an easy translation but it seemed to take forever for my mind to process it. Someone was telling me to be quiet. To be quiet because the King's soldiers were near.

The King. Which king? The last king to rule France was Louis Philippe I. That would mean we were back sometime between 1830 and 1850. But why would the king's soldiers be after someone in the sewers? Unless this wasn't the 19th century and it was another king altogether.

But which king? Then my mind snapped back to Aeden and the silence that replaced her scream. I moved as quickly as I could to the spot where I last heard her voice.

Chapter Eleven: Aeden

The small walkway that jutted out from the walls of the sewer was wet and uneven. I couldn't get a footing. Worse, the wall behind me was slippery. No place to get a hold. As I tried to stand, my feet kept slipping out from underneath me. There was a faint light in the distance that seemed to flicker. Bad electrical connection? I didn't think so. I think we got flipped back further in time. Before electricity. So much for my brother's perfect planning.

I tried to keep myself from falling long enough for Ryn to reach me, but it was impossible. My feet slid forward until I was at the edge of the walkway. My body started to slip and I screamed. I could feel the back of the wall graze my thighs as I sank closer and closer to the moving water. Water that I could only assume was sewage. Again, I opened my mouth to scream but someone's hand covered it before I could catch my breath. Then, whoever it was leaned forward, and with the other hand, grabbed me from the waist and pulled me back to the ledge. I turned and could see that it was a male figure, slightly taller than Ryn.

"Tais-toi! Les soldats du roi."

All of it was incomprehensible. But the voice was urgent. This was no small talk. Again, he spoke.

"Tais-toi! Les soldats du roi. Suivez –moi!"

"Oui!"

It was Ryn. Ryn saying "yes." One of the few words I understood. I just wished I knew what we were doing. The man kept his hand firmly clasped to my arm as we started down the walkway. Behind me, I could feel movement and a warm, familiar breath against my neck. I slowed down to listen carefully as my brother whispered, his words barely audible against the sound of the water and the scuttling of our feet.

"Just follow him. And no talking. No English."

The scant light in the distance was getting closer, and its source confirmed all my fears. It was the flame at the tip of a long wooden torch that was propped against the tunnel wall. A torch. Time before electricity. Time before lanterns. Or maybe it was just an anomaly. I tried not to dwell on it as the man's grasp slid further down my arm to my wrist. He still would not let go.

"Par ici. Soyez prudent. Regardez vous marchez."

I understood the last word. *Marchez.* Something about walking. It felt as if my feet had no connection to my body, but somehow I kept up with him. Knowing that Ryn was right behind me made it bearable. But we never got close to the flame. A few seconds later, the man put his hand on my head, forcing me to bend down and keep walking. We were entering a lower chamber. I wanted to warn Ryn but he told me not to speak in English. Then I remembered. I knew the word for "duck." Or at least I knew how it appeared on a menu.

"Le canard," I uttered softly.

Too late. A thud and I knew my brother's head had hit the wall.

"Imbecile," I heard him sputter as he caught up to me in the narrower tunnel.

The stench was becoming unbearable, as was the tight grip on my wrist. Still, if we were to get out of here, we had to follow whoever was holding me by the arm.

We moved quickly and wordlessly. The grip that was tightening on my wrist gave me a strange reassurance that everything was going to be all right. Someone knew where they were going. Someone knew the passages underground. All I had to do was allow myself to be led.

The floor in the narrower tunnel was not as wet. Easier to maneuver. And it appeared to be better lit even though I couldn't see any torches. I reached my free hand to touch the wall and it was dry. We were moving further away from the sewage and seepage. Then, in an instant, he had let go. No one was holding my arm. I reached forward to see if I could get ahold of him. Grab him by his shirt or something. My arms flailed about in the darkness. The man was gone. I spun around to reach for my brother but he wasn't there either.

Chapter Twelve:

Ryn

Le canard? Roast duck? What on earth was Aeden trying to tell me? Then, it dawned on me. Duck! She was trying to use a verb, but instead she picked a noun. It wasn't her fault but I felt like clobbering her altogether, especially when I smacked my head right into the wall.

The tunnel was tight and suffocating, not to mention that it stunk like a cesspit. Still, it was dry. I had to keep pace with her and whoever was leading us out of there. The light was faint, but not enough to indicate where we were going. We were relying on someone we'd never met and the last time I did that...well, I didn't even want to think about it.

Aeden kept getting further ahead of me. Damn it. It was impossible to see in the dark.

Then, out of nowhere. Aeden's voice. In a zillion decibels.

"Ryn! Ryn! Where are you?"

"Shh...I'm right behind you. What happened to the guy who was taking us out of here?"

"I don't know. All of a sudden he was gone."

"There must be another passage. Start feeling the walls for an opening, and for heaven's sake, stop yelling."

"The only thing I feel is wall. Rock solid wall."

"Aeden, don't just touch one spot on the wall. Move your hand all over for an opening. He had to have gone through an opening."

All I needed was for her to start freaking out again and screaming. If there were soldiers in this sewer tunnel we didn't need to be escorted anywhere by them.

"Well, have you found anything in front of you?" I whispered.

"Not exactly. But..."

"But what?"

"Feels like something wooden on the wall."

"Aeden, it's probably a door. See if you can find a latch or knob."

The tunnel was too narrow for me to get in front and see for myself, so I just held my breath and waited.

A slow creak and I knew she had succeeded.

"You found it. Go on through."

"The door opened, Ryn," her muffled voice replied. "But I wasn't the one who opened it."

And then, the other voice. The one from before.

"Attendez! J'ai besoin de vous assurer qu'il est sécuritaire. Maintenat, suivez-moi."

Aeden moved quickly through the door and I wasted no time following her. The guy indicated it was safe. He had to make sure. That's why he kept Aeden waiting. But safe from what? The soldiers? What could they possibly want with us... unless... unless that stinky kid in front of the pyramid forced us back to the worst possible time in the history of France.

I grimaced as I followed Aeden. It was a staircase. A narrow stone staircase. And there was light at the top. Grey murky light. I thought the odor would dissipate as we continued to climb but it didn't, and I began to realize why. *Holy crap. This stench is embedded in our clothes. I am a walking cesspit.*

Dusk. The grey murky light was dusk. I could see the outline of three or four story buildings in front of us. Close together. But there were no lights. Just flickering. *Candles. Candlelight was the only light that could be seen in some of the windows. What the heck year was this?*

The guy wasted no time racing across the alleyway and motioning Aeden and me to follow.

"Dépêchez-vous!"

Even Aeden knew it meant hurry, and we did. Across the alley and into a side door. Up four flights of old wooden stairs without stopping to catch our breath. Then through another doorway and up another flight of stairs.

"Dépêchez-vous!"

The guy was scared. Frantic. And his fear was becoming contagious. We pounded up the steps as if the wooden planks were about to eat our heels.

A quick pull on the doorknob and we were ushered into a dark room with a sloped ceiling. A bleak room whose only illumination was the fading light from the sunset outside. There was a word for rooms like this in the attics of old French buildings. Rooms that housed artists, musicians and writers. But that was another time. Another century. This garret wasn't housing any writers. Just the guy who led us out of the sewer and into what? He held his index finger across his lips, signaling for us to keep still.

We watched as he crossed the room to peer out of the tiny window to the street below. I walked quietly behind him. And even though the window was caked with dirt, I could easily discern the shape that stood directly in front of me. Past the houses, past the street, framing the night sky. A fortress whose fate would change the 18th century forever. The Bastille. And Aeden and I had just walked into the darkest part of history on a sunny morning in front of the Louvre.

Damn that rotten, incorrigible little kid!

Chapter Thirteen: *Aeden*

I could tell something was wrong the minute Ryn looked out the window. He didn't have to say a word. The guy said something to him, then left the room for a few minutes, returning with a small lit candle, carefully cradled in a cupped holder. His absence gave me enough time to speak in the only language I understood.

"You know something Ryn. You know where we are and when. Tell me."

"We're near the Bastille. Before the French Revolution. That's why the guy who lives here was so freaked out about the soldiers in the sewer."

"The French Revolution? That was like...what? Hundreds of years ago... Oh my God, Ryn. The French Revolution? Peasants rioting in the streets? That revolution? I told you we had to worry about our clothes. But you said we'd only be off by a few days or weeks. Not centuries. What's going to happen when it gets to be daylight and the guy takes a good look at us?"

"If anyone should be worrying about clothing Aeden, it's me. My clothes are putrid. Didn't you get a good whiff in the tunnel? Look, I'll try to explain that our clothes are wet and maybe this guy can find us something to wear. Now just calm down. Besides, we need to find out who he is and why he helped us out of the sewer. Remember, don't say a word. Not even *oui*. Okay?"

I nodded and sat down on a hard chair against the wall. Seconds later, the guy re-entered the room carrying the candlestick. He said something to us and Ryn responded. I just stared at them, acting as if I knew what was going on. Then a fast paced conversation followed. My eyes darted from my brother to the guy and back again. In the semi-darkness I could see that the guy was probably in his late teens or early twenties. He was tall and muscular, with straight brown hair. And there was something else. Something familiar that I couldn't begin to place.

For a moment the guy laughed, and then his voice got serious again. I was astonished that my brother could keep up with him, but Ryn had real motivation to learn the language. Mademoiselle Claudine. I was content to struggle along with Señor Lopez in Spanish One and began to wonder if I had made the right choice.

Then the guy pointed to the scrunchy ribbon that held my hair back and Ryn said something. Ribbons? The guy was interested in ribbons? None of this made sense. Then he walked over to a small wooden chest and opened it, motioning for me to do something with the contents.

Ryn responded and the guy left the room, his footsteps racing down the stairs. I grabbed my brother by the arm but before I could say anything, he spoke.

"Listen Aeden, we don't have much time. That guy's name is Michel and he thinks we're part of a secret society that's killing off the aristocracy one by one. That's why he saved us from the soldiers in the sewer. He thought we were being pursued."

"What gave him that idea?"

"Well, other than you screaming, he caught a glimpse of your hair ribbon. That's apparently the sign for others in this society. A red hair ribbon or red scarf."

"Is he killing off the aristocracy?"

"Don't know yet. Anyway, the chest he pointed to has old rags and old clothes. We need to change. Quickly."

"But we can't leave our clothes here. They're from another century."

"I know. I know. I'm gonna stink from kingdom come but we have no choice. Put a skirt or rags on over your jeans. Just pull the jeans up. Your clunky brown shoes actually look okay."

"These are Doc Martens. They cost me a month's allowance."

"Terrific, Aeden. The good news is that he made the fashion page for the 1700s. Now hurry up!"

Ryn grabbed some old material from the chest and tossed it my way. It was easier for him. His jeans were black and so filthy that they actually looked ageless. Same with his sneaks. He just threw a white shirt on over his sweatshirt and he was all set.

"So now what?" I asked.

But before Ryn could answer, Michel had opened the door and motioned for us to follow him.

"Suivez-moi. Dépêchez – vous!"

I started to leave the room when I noticed something written on the wall by the door. It was a list of names. Some of them had been crossed out.

Anjou
Artois
Beaulieu
Chastain
Dampierre
Dreux
Richelieu
Vermandois

And there, in the middle, was the one name I recognized. *Chastain.* My mother's maiden name. Uncle Henri's name. And it wasn't crossed out. Not yet.

Chapter Fourteen:

Ryn

This Michel guy was a full blown killer of the aristocracy all right. He had names. He had lists. And he had friends. Lots of them. I didn't want to tell Aeden just yet 'cause I knew she'd go bonkers.

"It's the only way France will ever change," he told me. "Ending the aristocracy one by one." Good thing Aeden didn't understand the conversation.

"So," Michel continued as I listened intently, "how many names have you crossed off your list?"

"My sister and I are new to this," I replied. "It's overwhelming for her and she doesn't speak much."

"As long as she can move a dagger across the throat, she does not have to speak at all."

Yeah, darn good thing Aeden didn't understand a word. But she was catching on, especially when Michel motioned for us to follow him down the stairs.

With the exception of a few torch lights in the entrances of the nearby buildings, the street was pitch black. Pitch black and deadly quiet. So quiet that the sound of Michel's soft voice seemed to thunder in my ears.

"It is a good night for Beaulieu, but we must move quickly."

Was he about to murder some guy? I really didn't want to stick around, but then again, Aeden and I didn't need to be his next victims. I figured we might be able to dart away if we were fast enough, but to where...I had no idea. And no way to tell Aeden. So we kept pace with Michel as he rounded the corner of the block and followed another street. A sudden turn to the left and we were headed down a new street. Not as tight. The buildings stretched further away from each other. But in the darkness, they all seemed the same—iron gratings and wisps of candlelight.

"Through here," Michel said as he led us into an alleyway. Only this one was wider and I could see some sort of park at the end of it.

Well, this is it. He'll probably knife us and leave us here. A good night for the Beaulieu and the riff-raff from the sewers.

I kept myself at an arm's length from him with Aeden right behind. But he showed no sign of wanting to stab us in an alleyway. And after all, he could have done that in his own alleyway and saved himself some time.

Okay. So it's just the Beaulieu who are going to have the surprise of their lives.

We crossed a cobblestone road to the park. Just shadows of trees and bushes as we followed the walkway over a small bridge. My eyes were getting used to the dark and I could see houses a few feet away. Not buildings. Not apartments. Houses. Large separate houses with ornate wrought iron balconies.

"Number 179, on the right," Michel whispered. "We need to move quickly."

I usually like to know what I'm doing, or at least have a reasonable idea. Were we going to knock on the door? *Doubtful.* Break a window? *Too loud.* This clandestine killing of the aristocracy was not in the French IV Syllabus at Riverdale High School. I just had to watch and see what Michel had in mind.

He motioned for us to walk to the side of the house where some taller trees lined a garden pathway. There were two stories, well, three if you count the attic area. On the bottom, tall windows with decorative grating opened into large rooms that could easily be seen from outside. Sconces and candlelight illuminated them. The bedrooms had to be upstairs.

It's always the bedrooms. They always want to murder people in their bedrooms. Just like poor Uncle Henri.

Just then, Michel turned and spoke directly to Aeden.

"Je me tiendrai sur la rambarde et vous donner un ascenseur. Un coup de pouce. Vous aurez besoin de monter au haut de la fenetre et l'ouvrir."

He was telling her that he'd give her a boost so she could climb from one story to the next and open the top window. He might as well have told her that he was going to launch her into outer space for all she understood. I had to act fast.

"I'll do it," I said in flawless French. "My sister won't be strong enough to open a window. Give me a boost. You can help her up next."

Michel didn't argue as I stepped into his clasped hands and reached for the bottom of the second story railing. *Why is everything always a foot away from where it needs to be?* I leaned closer and stretched as hard as I could.

Thought every muscle in my arms would tear but somehow I got to the railing and managed to hoist myself up. Standing on the balcony, it was easier to grab Aeden once Michel gave her a boost. Yeah, she figured it out. But Michel? How the heck was he gonna get up here? And he better not tell me to go kill some aristocrat for him. I was about to say something when he stepped away from the windows and toward the trees.

You'd better not be leaving us here. You'd better...

And then I saw what he was doing. He climbed that tree as if it were a ladder, balancing himself carefully on a large limb. But the balcony was a good four or five feet from where he stood, and even the best jumpers can't always make that distance, let alone at night, in the dark, on a tree.

"Grab my arms," he shouted, "and I can pull myself up."

And even though his words were in French, I think my sister understood exactly what he planned to do. She edged forward as well, in case I missed.

Chapter Fifteen: Aeden

I never had anyone grab me by the waist and hoist me up in the air. Well, maybe as a baby or toddler, but I don't remember. It was dark and he couldn't see the jeans underneath the material I had wrapped around me. Then again, I don't think he was looking or even cared. He was focused. Driven. I didn't need to understand French to figure that out. And I didn't need French to figure out what we were about to do.

Ryn grabbed my arms and I was able to get a good footing on the railing of the balcony. Breaking and entering. That's what we were about to do. Well, technically *entering* if the window was open. I wondered which name this was. Which house? All I could think about were those names etched on the wall. And the ones that were crossed out? Did that mean they were already dead? Murdered?

There was no time to think. Michel was about to jump from his position on the tree limb to the balcony railing. He had to be fast. Fast and agile enough to make the distance. Ryn could grab him, providing he was in reach. But there was no way of figuring out where the guy's arms were going to wind up. I only knew that Michel had a better chance if Ryn and I were both there. I stepped forward and held my breath.

It was fast. A swoosh and Michel's arms were gripped tight to the lower part of the balcony rail. All he needed to do was pull himself up. It should have taken less than a second. But there was no movement. Even in the dark I could see Michel's hands holding the railing. Then why didn't he move?

"Oui est la? Qui va la?"

We held still. Someone was below us. They must have heard a sound and came outside to check. That's why Michel didn't dare make a move. I inhaled slowly, scared to release any breath. Ryn was immobile, too. Small beads of sweat started to form at the base of my hairline. How long would we stand here?

"Il n'y a rien. Peut-etre que c'etait un chien ou un chat."

And then the voice disappeared. In the silence I could hear whoever it was walking slowly back to the front of the house.

"At last," Michel whispered as he pulled himself up to the balcony, "they've gone. They thought the noise was a dog or cat, never would guess it was a sewer rat!"

He placed both of his hands on the window pane and slowly glided it up. An easy entrance. Bending his head, he stepped inside, and then motioned for Ryn and me to follow.

We stepped inside a dark room whose only illumination came from the faint light under the doorway. I could see the shape of a large bed in the middle of the room and an armoire directly across from it. Michel said something quietly to Ryn and we moved closer to the walls, edging our way towards the door. My hands were shaking and it felt as if my entire body was drenched in sweat. We were going to kill someone. Stab them. Leave the mark of the fleur-de-lis on their neck.

I knew this was how history played out. How a revolution got started. But it was always in books and movies, not a few feet down the hall, in another room, with an unsuspecting victim.

My knees wobbled and I needed to lean against something. Carefully, silently, I stepped next to the armoire and moved my hands behind my back to reach for the wall. But what stood behind me was anything but beams and wood. I could feel the pulse of someone breathing. The slow inhale and exhale meant that we weren't alone. I wasn't about to take a chance. I moved forward, ready to elbow him, but he was faster, grabbing my forearms and pulling me closer to his chest. The scream that was about to leave my mouth never happened. The person who was standing directly behind me bent forward and spoke softly in my ear.

"Tout va bien."

It was close enough to the little Spanish I knew to realize he was telling me that everything was okay. How could everything be okay when we were about to murder someone?

Then I heard Michel speak.

"Alain? Alain c'est que vous?"

They knew each other. The conversation was brief but I was sure Ryn understood every word.

"It is done, Michael. No need to stay. The last of the Beaulieus can now rot away in hell with the rest of the aristocracy."

"And the others on the list?"

"Chastain is next. Perhaps I should leave that one to you."

"It would be my pleasure."

Then Michel muttered something to us and the next thing I knew, we were climbing down from the balcony. Alain and Michel first. They were fast. Agile. And apparently used to the contortions our bodies had to make as we edged over railings and jumped to the ground.

As we started for the street, Ryn reached out his hand and placed it on Michel's chest. He, in turn, stopped walking and listened to the one sentence my brother said. The one sentence that would change everything for us.

"Go home, Michel. Rest assured that we will kill the Chastains."

Chapter Sixteen:

Ryn

Even in the semi-darkness of the street, I could see Aeden's eyes widen as she tried desperately to figure out what Michel and Alain were telling me. Alain spoke first, putting a hand on my shoulder and staring directly into my face. Like Michel, he was tall, thin and wiry.

"The sewers are crawling with soldiers as you well know. Your only choice is to use the catacombs to reach the Chastains. The authorities have not bothered to look for us beneath the churches. But that could change. You must be careful. So much depends upon your success tonight."

"I understand," I replied, trying not to give any indication that I didn't have a clue where the damn catacombs were, let alone the Chastain residence. Then Michel spoke.

"We will walk you as far as the church. Once inside, you'll find your way below. Follow the hallway until you get to the first quarry. Count three quarries and then look for a small opening. You must crawl through it to reach the passageway out. Torches are always lit for the dead so you'll find your way."

Before I could say anything, Michel continued.

"14 Rue Daguerre. And bid the Chastains farewell for me."

Rue Daguerre. Number 14. That's what we had to look for once we got out of the catacombs. Rue Daguerre, number 14. *We'd be walking into our own history. Geez. I'm not sure I can handle this. And if I so much as breathe wrong, I'll change it. And then what?* I tried to act as nonchalant as possible as Michel and Alain walked with us to the church. Nonchalant all right. Nonplussed. As if I go around knifing people in the throat all the time...

If Aeden had any indication where we were going, she didn't let on. I figured I'd explain everything once we got into the church and were left on our own. She'd be fine going into the church. It was the stuff underneath it that was going to scare the living crap out of us. We just didn't know it yet.

I don't know what I expected, but the building was small. A stone structure with a wooden door and a few long windows on either side. The trees that surrounded it made it seem even creepier than it was. Like something out of a dark fairytale. As Aeden and I started to walk in, Michel grabbed my arm and spoke.

"Why so intent on killing the Chastains my friend? You seem so eager."

"Eager, my-you-know-what," I thought to myself. "If you really knew what I had in mind, that fleur-de-lis would be carved on my throat." But I couldn't let on. Instead, I let the air out of my mouth slowly and replied.

"Our father died in the Bastille. From lies the Chastains told. They killed him with their words. Now I do the same with my dagger."

I hoped I sounded convincing enough, considering that I had no dagger. No knife. No nothing. Not even a pin. Still, they didn't know. Then Alain spoke as I opened the door to the church, letting out the faint light from the few remaining candles that were still lit.

"Remember, pull his head back by the hair and slit his throat with one move. Be quick. Be careful. We shall meet again. Our duty to France has just begun."

"Yes, you be careful, too," I said.

And then I closed the door behind us, motioning for Aeden to keep quiet until I was sure they had gone.

It was more a chapel than a church, and for a minute it reminded me of that silly little game we played when we were kids-opening our fingers, moving them back and forth to the rhyme, *"Here's the church and there's the steeple. Open the door, and here's the people."* But Aeden and I were the only ones in the narrow building. Even in the dim light, I could tell that no one else was here.

Votive candles were stacked in neat rows on both of the side walls. Someone must have been here earlier to light them. They probably lit them and left. The pews didn't look the least bit comfortable. Just hard, ordinary benches. I wouldn't hang around either. Then it dawned on me. Were other people down in the catacombs too? I pulled Aeden by the arm and yanked her into one of the pews. I didn't need to see the look on her face to know that she was really pissed.

"What on earth is going on, Ryn? First we scale up someone's house to do God knows what and then we don't do it, and next we hurry back with another guy who was hiding in the house, and then we're suddenly on our own in this little church. They didn't bring us here to pray. WHAT'S GOING ON?"

"You don't need to go off and have a major freak-out, Aeden. Just listen. Then if you want to get yourself all worked up and crazy, be my guest!"

She stopped talking long enough for me to explain, or at least start to explain.

"You were right about the names on the wall. Each name is an aristocrat and one by one, Michel and his secret society of throat slitting killers are murdering them. For France, by the way, in case you were wondering. But when we got to the Beaulieu residence, this guy Alain had already slashed Monsieur Beaulieu's throat. No sense sticking around. So we left. And next on the list was the name Chastain."

Aeden gasped and I continued to speak.

"Okay, so you figured that out. I had to convince Michel and Alain that we were going to murder Monsieur Chastain in order to stop them from doing it. That's why we're here. This is the short-cut to the Chastain mansion."

"We're in a little church. What kind of short-cut is that?"

"The short-cut is below us. We need to walk through some catacombs."

"I'll kill you, Ryn. I swear, I'll kill you. I'm not walking through catacombs. You're not making me walk through old mounds of dead people. It's not happening. We can take the long way to the Chastain mansion."

"We can't, Aeden. The streets are full of soldiers, and besides, we don't know how to get there. I only have directions from the exit once we leave the catacombs. If we step outside right now we could be arrested."

"For what?"

"Does it matter? They don't seem to ask too many questions around here, so I suggest you stop complaining and start looking for a doorway."

"I mean it, Ryn. I don't want to walk through dead people."

"You're not going to walk through dead people. Well, technically, maybe, yes... but it's just their bones. Just old bones. Nothing to be scared of. Come on, we don't have much time."

"I hate you, Ryn. I hate you."

"Fine, just look for a doorway."

Chapter Seventeen: *Aeden*

The sewer couldn't be helped. We landed there. But Ryn could have done something about the catacombs. He could have made some excuse to not have us go through there, but he didn't. And I may never speak to him again. Ever!

Off to the side of the altar was a small door. An "Alice in Wonderland" type door that we had to crawl through. And then, a long, winding staircase that got narrower and narrower as we made our way down. Flickering torchlight filled the staircase with smoke and dust. Still, it was better than nothing. The thought of absolute darkness unnerved me more than the remains of the dead that we were about to see. I kept one hand on Ryn's shirt, even though I wasn't speaking to him. And it wouldn't have mattered. He was too busy counting the steps.

"One hundred seventeen, one hundred eighteen...for crying out loud, how many damn steps are there?"

"Don't ask me, Ryn. This is all your fault. And by the way, I'm not talking to you unless I have to."

"One hundred twenty-four...grow up Aeden. One hundred twenty-five...hey, it looks like I can see the bottom. The floor. It's a long rounded tunnel with brickwork on the top."

We reached bottom at 130 steps. It was like descending into a deep well. I hated to think about the climb back up. Someone had lit torches along the walls. Not many, but enough to cast an eerie light on the place. Not that it needed it. It was scary enough. Ryn headed straight down the tunnel and I made sure not to let him out of my sight.

"We have to count three quarries, Aeden, and then look for a small opening in the wall."

"Quarries?"

"Yeah, you know. Quarries. Where they excavate and pile up stuff."

"Say it Ryn. Dead bodies. We're looking for piles of dead bodies."

"I think the bones are categorized, actually."

"WHAT?"

As if the thought of hundreds of skeletons wasn't disgusting enough, now the bones were all supposed to be separated out. I didn't say anything else and just kept walking.

"First quarry," Ryn announced. "See, it's not that bad. Just a pile of long bones wedged into a deep crevice in this tunnel. Think of it like logs."

"I'm not thinking about it at all. Just keep walking."

The tunnel curved and we found ourselves in a tightly wound passageway with no torches. Still, we could see the light ahead of us from another area. Then, more twists and turns. It was getting darker and the only way to get further ahead was to touch both sides of the wall.

"Watch it, Aeden. The floor is getting uneven."

Sure enough, it was like we were walking on cobblestones. And maybe we were for all I knew. And it was getting colder, too. I hadn't noticed the chill at first, but this part of the tunnel was certainly colder. The passageway seemed to contort and thread like a funhouse. But this was no Disney World. A few feet later and we didn't have to reach our hands to touch the walls. We were wedged against them as we tried to move forward.

A sudden turn and nothing but pitch black in front of us.

"Keep moving, Aeden."

"Like what else am I supposed to do?"

Another quick curve and we could make out the faint light emanating from the ceiling.

"It's floorboards. Way up high. We're under some sort of structure. Maybe another church," I said.

The tunnel widened and I could feel some of the tension in my body releasing. Ryn was back on task as well. Giving orders.

"Two more quarries to go. Keep looking for them."

I felt disoriented and light headed. Maybe from being so far underground. But not so confused that I didn't see the enormous stack of skulls that lined the floor from top to bottom as we made one final turn. My shriek echoed in the chamber, bouncing from one hollow skull to the next. I screamed and screamed until I had no breath left.

Ryn's arms shook my shoulders. He spoke softly as if the least little sound would cause an avalanche of skulls. An underground avalanche that would claim its next victims.

Chapter Eighteen:
Ryn

You'd think I did this deliberately to torture her. Good grief. Aeden needed to get a grip. Calm herself down and be rational. It was just skulls. The people were already dead. It wasn't as if they were some sort of Hollywood zombies coming after us. I swear, her scream sucked the air out of the place.

"Relax, Aeden. Nothing's going to happen. Just keep walking. Only one more quarry to go."

The third quarry was just a few feet ahead. I could see it from where I was standing. And it was weird. No rhyme. No reason. No order. Just a mish-mosh of bones and skulls mixed in and piled up until they reached the ceiling. Next to them, a carefully carved stone with the following inscription:

Ossements deposes en Avril 1786

Just like that. *Bones deposited in April, 1786.* Well, at least we knew one thing. It was after 1786 and before 1789 or the Bastille wouldn't be standing. It could be three years or three days before the revolution. We had no way of knowing. At least not then.

Aeden stood in front of the sign and touched the date with her hand.

"Come on, that's the last quarry. No more scary stuff. Okay? Now all we need to do is find a small opening in the wall."

"How small?"

"Now how should I know? I imagine small enough to be somewhat obscure but big enough for us to crawl through. All right?"

Aeden just stood there.

"Look, I don't like this either. You think I like the fact that my clothes smell from sewer and stink and I'll probably never get the stench out of my jeans? And God knows what's on the walls that we don't see. For all I know we could be covered with all sorts of unspeakable insects and worms and vermin and..."

And then I was sorry I said anything at all. Aeden went berserk.

"You think there's bugs on us? Get them off me. Get them off me!"

She started wiping her sleeves, shaking her head and stomping her feet. I had to think fast.

"It's too dry in here for bugs. Really. I was only trying to make a point. Now cut it out. The sooner we get the heck out of here, the better. Now start looking for that opening."

We walked slowly, eyeing both sides of the tunnel so we wouldn't miss anything. I don't know why I thought the opening would be at eye level but it wasn't and that's why we missed it at first. We just dead-ended against a cold stone wall. Aeden's voice was like an electric current running through the place.

"It's not here! It's not here! Oh my God, we've got to go back past the skulls and climb all those stairs again!"

"It's here, Aeden. We just missed it. We need to turn around and head back to the last quarry. This time, edge yourself against one side of the tunnel and I'll do the same on the other. Move your feet along the bottom to feel for an opening. Okay?"

"Yeah," Aeden sighed. "Okay."

We walked quietly. The only sound was the scuffle of our feet as they scraped against the uneven floor.

I didn't want to give in to my sister's panic but I was getting freaked out as well. *What if there was no opening. Then she'd be right. We'd have to go all the way back. And then what? Get caught by soldiers?* I tried not to think about it. Funny, when you stop thinking about something that's exactly when it happens. My foot skidded into hard brick and I almost fell forward.

"It's here Aeden! The opening! On the bottom of the wall!"

Bending down, I could see that it was a pretty narrow space. We'd have to crawl on the floor to worm our way into it. I tried not to think about what we were touching but Aeden wasn't making it any easier.

"You mean we've got to get down on the ground and use our elbows to crawl in here? I'm not the freaking white rabbit!"

"No, but Alice crawled into enough places and you can do it, too."

"Alice was fictional. Make-believe. And she wasn't worried about dead things and sewer stuff!"

"Just do it, Aeden. I'm going first and you'd better be right behind me."

The space was tight and I kept taking deep breaths as I pushed myself further and further into the crawl space. Like the rest of the catacombs, the tunnel curved and my body seemed to bank against one side of the wall; but then, as I moved forward, I could see the opening. It was lit. Torches on the walls and a wide, clear space.

"It's not very far," I said. "I can see the opening."

As Aeden wedged her way forward, I could feel her hands occasionally bumping into my feet. Normally I'd tell her to keep her distance but this was one time when I really needed to know that she was right behind me.

"That stinking hard floor," I said as I got up slowly and brushed off whatever loose dirt was on my clothing. "My knees are killing me."

"Give me a hand, Ryn. All my clothes have bunched up and I keep stepping on them."

We walked a few feet away from the opening and gave our eyes a moment to get used to the new tunnel. It seemed large and round with only one way out. A smaller channel that veered off to the side. And for some reason, it appeared to be better lit than the ones we just came through.

"Guess this is it, Aeden. Let's go."

Just then, the light in the new tunnel started to strobe. At first small flickers and then something out of a 1970's disco. Bouncing light. Waving light. Bright light.

Aeden and I approached it slowly, as if the light itself could blind us. But it wasn't the light we needed to worry about. In front of us were at least a dozen people. And they were waving flashlights and laughing.

Chapter Nineteen: Aeden

"We're back, Ryn. We're back!" I was so excited to see people in jeans and hoodies, with water bottles and flashlights that I just started to race over to them.

"NO!" my brother screamed as he grabbed me from the nape of my neck. "Don't go there!"

"But it may be our only chance back."

"It's a time rift, Aeden. A small ripple. But if we go back, then someone is going to kill Monsieur Chastain and we won't exist. We disappear as if we were never born, because we won't be born. Don't you understand? We have to warn him. Prevent him from being murdered. If Monsieur Chastain becomes a fleur-de-lis victim, then our great, great, great grandfather and the whole damn family line just goes up in smoke. It's that time-space paradox. We can't go back."

I was tired of listening to my brother so I squirmed, but he tightened his grip on my neck with the one hand and held me by the waist with the other.

"I get it, Ryn. You can let me go."

I was close enough to read the label on one of the water bottles. *Dasani*. All I had to do was make a quick run for it. I could almost taste the cool water on my mouth. No pond water. Not scummy ground water, but clear, purified 21st century water. My time. My water.

My heel caught Ryn by surprise on his shin and I started for the water. The kid who was holding it would surely give me a sip. But my brother was fast and he managed to get a good hold of my shirt just as the lights started to flicker even more.

White. Yellow. White. Blue. Flickering. Bouncing. Waving. The intensity of color knew no bounds. And then, it was as if the walls started to move with the light. I could still feel Ryn's grip, but he didn't have to worry. I wasn't about to make a move.

In a flash, it was over. No more lights. No more people. No ice cold Dasani bottles. Only darkness and the faint glow from a distant wall torch.

I pounded my brother in the arm as I spoke. Each word came out as a sob, a choking, air-grasping sob that wouldn't stop.

"You've ruined it. We'll never get back. What if that was our last chance? Our only chance. And now it's done. We'll die in this godforsaken century. I hate you, Ryn. I mean it. I hate you."

"You're alive because of me, Aeden. So hate me all you want. Just listen. That rift in time would have changed everything. We wouldn't exist. We have to make sure that the Chastains are alive long enough for our great, great, ...you know, grandfather to be born. Or we won't be."

"But what if it really is too late and we won't get back?"

"We will. We just don't understand all the scientific principles of time right now. Think of it like an eclipse. Years and years ago people were petrified of eclipses. They thought it was the end of the world. They didn't understand that it was just the shadow of the moon as the moon passed between the sun and the earth. Years from now scientists will have a better handle on the time-space continuum. And you'll see that once something gets moved out of its own time, like us, the natural result will be to eventually move that object back to where it belonged. The natural order of things has to be restored."

"And what about Uncle Henri? We were supposed to go back, watch his apartment and find out who killed him. Now we can't even do that."

"Something in this century may lead us to a clue later on. You just need to trust the order of the universe."

I don't remember when I stopped crying, but when I did, the stillness in the catacomb tunnel was the most frightening thing of all. But if I had known right there and then that Ryn was just feeding me a pack of lies, well... that would have scared me more than all the skulls in the entire Paris underground.

Chapter Twenty: *Ryn*

It was bad enough dealing with bossy know-it-all Aeden. But overly emotional, "cry-at-the-drop-of-a-hat" Aeden was really getting to me. I didn't know how much more of it I could stand without losing it all together and saying something I'd regret. Thankfully, a stairwell to the passage out of the catacombs was visible once we stepped further into the large room.

"Look Aeden. Just past the rounded archways is a staircase. And there's a torch on the wall next to it. We've found our way out."

Aeden walked directly to the stairs and looked up.

"The only light is the torch. Once we start climbing, we won't be able to see anything."

"Won't be able to see anything? That's the least of our problems. It's like a million steps up. My legs are going to get shin splints. This absolutely sucks." That's what I wanted to say. But I didn't. Because if I did, Aeden would start that crying all over again. So instead, I said something else.

"It won't matter if we can't see anything. It's just steps. We just keep climbing. Eventually the steps will end and we'll be back on level ground."

"In another church?"

"I don't know. Maybe. But it will be real close to the Chastain residence. That's what Michel and Alain said."

"I hate them, too."

"Great, Aeden. Don't friend them on Facebook. Now come on."

Another spiral staircase. This time with higher steps and I knew it would be tough going for both of us.

"If your legs get tired, just tell me and we'll take a break, okay?"

"What if I get dizzy?"

"Then we'll take a break," I said as we started up the never ending spiral of triangular steps. But the thought of my sister losing her balance began to bother me. If she were to wobble and plunge, there'd be no way back.

"Aeden, would you rather go in front of me so if you really felt dizzy I could grab you?"

"No, I'll be fine. Besides, then we'd both fall. You go first."

The torch light from below lasted longer than I expected. And even though it was dim, we were able to keep climbing without a problem. But dim became faint and faint became dark as we reached the mid-point of our ascent. I didn't want to tell Aeden that I had a really terrifying thought. What if someone were climbing down the stairs? We'd never see them and they'd bump right into us. My mind started to picture all sorts of horrific outcomes and then I realized something. Our footsteps made a noise. A fairly loud noise in the narrow stairwell. If anyone was on the way down, we'd hear them long before they reached us. Geez, I hated the darkness. I needed to get the heck out of there before my mind conjured up another nightmare.

I didn't want to count the steps this time. What was the point? I just keep going. Reminding myself to lift one foot, then the other. And I swear, the steps were getting taller and taller with each curve in the spiral.

"Can you see anything yet?"

"You're right behind me. You see the same thing I do. Nothing. Just keep walking."

Another curve. Another circle.

"What about now?"

"If I saw something Aeden, I'd tell you. But put your hand on the wall. The stone is dry. That means we're more than halfway there. Remember? The walls got moist as we headed down. Just keep moving."

The monotonous thud of our feet on the steps began to feel like a slow torture. I took a deep breath and kept climbing. But something was different. The air. It wasn't stagnant or moist. It was crisp and I could make out the smell of smoke from somewhere in the distance.

"Do you smell it Aeden? Like a campfire or chimney? We're getting close."

Another few steps and I felt my head hit a grating.

"We're at the top but there's some sort of grating above us."

"Like a sewer?"

"Don't even say that. But, yeah. Like a sewer. It must open up somewhere for us to crawl out of."

Above us was the street. Or at least I thought it was the street. It was too dark to tell. I moved my hands across the grating until I felt a spot that was fairly wide. At least wide enough for me to wedge myself through.

"Aeden, I've got to boost myself up so take a step down slowly."

"If I step down I'm going to fall."

"Fine. But if I kick you in the head as I'm climbing up, you'll fall anyway."

I could hear her sigh as she moved down a step.

"As soon as I'm up, I'll reach down and pull you, Aeden. Just give me your hands as soon as I say so."

I'll never complain about doing pull-ups again in a P.E. class. I needed those muscles or I never would have made it. I just kept pulling my body up until my waist was level with the ground and I could lean far enough over to kick my leg onto the floor. It scraped the metal grating and tore my jeans, but hell, I was out!

Without stopping to look around, I leaned down and grabbed both of Aeden's arms, but she felt like dead weight.

"You've got to do something, Aeden. I just can't pull you up by myself."

"Like what?"

"I don't know. Use your legs to push off of a wall for momentum."

"How did you get out?"

"Grabbed the grating and did a pull-up."

"Let me try."

Sure enough, Aeden had the strength to do a quick pull-up. I had just enough seconds to get a decent grip and yank her up the rest of the way. I was so intent on getting her out that I didn't pay attention to anything else.

"Footsteps, Ryn. It's footsteps and they're coming from right behind us. On the stairwell. Someone was right behind us and we never heard a thing."

Everything seemed to snap at once. We were on a street, just like Michel had said. Minutes from the Chastain mansion. But who was behind us?

In the cool night air, with the distant smell of smoke, Aeden and I ran straight ahead. No choice. We had to put lots of distance between us and the footsteps.

Chapter Twenty-One: *Aeden*

Ryn kept running and I forced myself to keep up with him. My legs felt heavy and numb from climbing all those stairs. The worst part was that my clothes seemed to weigh a ton. I felt as if my body was about to crumble when Ryn finally slowed down. With a sharp motion of his hand, he pointed to a small alcove by the side of a large building.

"We can take a break for a few minutes, Aeden. I don't hear the footsteps."

"Soldiers, you think?"

"For all I know, it could have been Michel and Alain following us to make sure we do what we said we would."

"What *you* said we would."

"Yeah, whatever. Meanwhile, we need to check the street corners to see what street we're on. There's enough light from wall torches and candles that people still have burning in their windows."

"So, I'm looking for a street sign?"

"No, they didn't have street signs then. The house at the end of every city block had to have a carved sign on both sides indicating the two streets that it occupied. I think it was a law or something. So we'll take a look when we get to the next block. We need to find Rue Daguerre, number 14."

The more I rested, the stickier I felt. It was as if my hair was glued to my scalp. We wouldn't have to work at looking like street mongrels. We were.

Ryn took a deep breath and then resumed walking. Slower this time. When we reached the corner, the stone block numbers and name were clear. We were on the corner of Rue Liancourt and Rue Danville. My brother's voice was soft but clear.

"Let's keep going straight. Michel didn't say anything about back-tracking so we've got to be headed in the right direction."

Even in the semi-darkness I could see that the buildings were large and ornate. Each one, its own palace. No wonder the lower classes were about to revolt. I just kept walking.

"Rue Danville and Rue Daguerre!" Ryn's voice was almost too loud. "We found it. Rue

Daguerre. I don't know if number 14 is on the left or right, so we'll just go right and check the numbers."

If there were people following us, they were awfully quiet about it. We started down the street but could not find a single number on any of the buildings.

"Maybe we're not looking in the right place, Ryn," I said as I approached a fancy three story dwelling with gilded ironwork and two miniature trees on either side of the entrance, each one carefully shaped to perfection.

Then, I glanced up.

"Oh my God. Look at the carving above the entranceway. It says *HOTEL CHASTAIN*. This has got to be the house. But it says *Hotel*. I don't get it."

"It just means it's their mansion. Their residence. It's not like a Holiday Inn, Aeden. It's just their home and we found it."

"So now what do we do? We don't have a plan or anything. Are you just going to knock on the door and tell Monsieur Chastain that he's next on the list to get his throat cut? Because if that's what you're going to do, I don't think it's such a great idea."

"So what bright idea do you have?"

I didn't have an idea and there's nothing worse than telling someone that their plan stinks when you don't have anything else to offer. I just kept still and let Ryn finish talking.

"Didn't think so, Aeden. Just keep still and listen."

Next thing I knew, my brother was knocking on the door. Pounding, actually. Three loud bangs that hung in the air like the aftermath of a small explosion. I stood there, frozen; not knowing what to expect. Ryn, I'm sure, had rehearsed everything he was about to say, but he never got the chance.

A heavy-set elderly woman, still dressed in her night clothes and holding a candle, opened the door slowly. She didn't have to speak. We were immediately swept into her arms. At least Ryn knew what this was all about. I just played along.

"Anjenet! Renaud! What are you doing here? What on earth happened? You were supposed to be on your way to Normandy. Oh never mind. Come in. Come in. Just look at you. What a mess! You must be hungry. Tired. Oh my goodness!"

Then she stopped long enough to shout out some names.

"Simeon! Lizette! Your master and mistress have returned. Quick! At once! Get them settled. Something for them to eat. Then allow

them to wash and get some rest. Quick, I say. Quick!"

A boy and girl about our own age came rushing down the front staircase, words tumbling out of their mouths almost as fast as their feet on the steps. Ryn answered.

"Yes, abducted. But we are safe. My sister is too exhausted to speak. Too traumatized."

Within seconds, they were escorting us upstairs to our rooms. Well, Anjenet and Renaud's rooms. I didn't need to speak French to figure that they thought we were someone else. But Ryn only took a few steps before turning around and speaking to the woman who opened the door.

"It is urgent that I speak with mon père, Urgent!"

Then, the lady did something we never expected. She held Ryn close to her chest and started to cry.

"Your father, Monsieur Chastain. Your poor father....He has been arrested. Taken to the Bastille."

I didn't need a translator. Even I understood.

Chapter Twenty-Two: Aeden

I let myself fall asleep in the comfort of down bedding and warm blankets. The outline of ornately carved wooden pillars at the bottom of my canopy bed were the last thing I saw before I let my mind shut down. It was a dreamless, airy sleep with the prior events still fresh in my mind.

My servant, Lizette, brought me a tray of warm bread rolls, butter, cheeses, and assorted pieces of sweet meats that I didn't recognize. A small fragrant tea was also served. It was the first meal I had eaten since breakfast... Breakfast in another time, another place. I had absentmindedly stuffed a croissant in my mouth before Ryn and I were driven to the Louvre. But these rolls were different. Tastier somehow. Maybe it was because I was famished. I don't know. I just let the butter and cheeses melt into my mouth as I washed them down with the flowery tea.

Then Lizette left the room, only to return with a dressing gown. She spoke to me in short simple sentences but all I could do was nod. Then, she motioned for me to follow her into another suite. Scones on the walls illuminated a large room with a single bathtub in the middle. It was smaller than any bathtub I'd ever seen, but it was tall, so that if you were to rest your head against the back of the tub, your neck would be supported by the porcelain. I could see that she wanted me to bathe and I had no objections. The tub was filled with scented soap and the water felt comfortably hot to my touch.

Thankfully, there was a dressing area of sorts—a tall screen made out of silk or some other fabric. On it were painted birds and greenery. I immediately went behind the screen, took off my clothing and bundled it together so that the rags would cover my jeans. My shoes did not appear to be a concern. Maybe Ryn was right. Fashions come back and my shoes were first on the list.

Lizette helped me into the tub and bent down to wash me with a cloth. I shook my head no and she stepped back, giving me an odd look. Maybe Anjenet was bathed by her servants but a few minutes in a warm shower are usually enough for me. When I was done, she handed me a large towel and helped me out of the tub and into my dressing gown. I quickly grabbed my clothing from behind the screen and followed her back to the bedroom. Anjenet's bedroom. My bedroom.

It was only when I clutched the pile of old clothes to my chest, that Lizette said something that made me nervous. It wasn't as if I understood her, but something about the way she looked at me made me feel as if all my worst secrets were suddenly splashed all over the internet for the whole world to see.

I didn't say a word. How could I? Lizette helped me into the bed and watched as I placed the clothing on the small table next to the headboard. She walked over to the wall sconces and blew them out, one by one. Then, taking a candle from another stand, she left the room and closed the door.

Now it was morning. Daylight was just announcing itself through the thin veil of curtains that hung between the thicker, heavy drapes. I sat up and took a good look at my surroundings. It was impossible to see anything clearly at night. As I moved my head from side to side, taking in the entire room, I knew immediately why Monsieur Chastain was so loathed.

Opulence. Elegance. Indulgence. It was all there in my room, from the large dressing table with perfume bottles and porcelain figurines to the collection of handmade dolls whose outfits were sewn with jewels and gems. On another table was a small stand with jewelry. Two huge hand-painted armoires were opposite my bed. Even the pitcher of water that stood on one of my nightstands was elegant and framed in gold.

I walked cautiously to the window and peered out. A magnificent garden with sculpted bushes and graceful benches was all I could see. A few large trees gave enough shade to give the place a certain charm. It was early. Even the birds were quiet.

Turning away from the window, I opened the first armoire. Dresses. Skirts. Floor length gowns. Each one more embellished than the last. At the bottom of the cabinet were shoes of all colors and styles. Then, the next armoire. This one held wraps, more skirts, blouses and everyday clothing. Again, more shoes. I pulled open the smaller drawers inside the second armoire and saw undergarments. Fancy, frilly, uncomfortable underwear. No way. My sweaty underwear would have to do.

Trying not to give it too much thought, I slipped on my underwear and top. Then, I found a skirt from the armoire, some sort of stockings and a wrap that I threw over my shirt. The only dilemma I had was my jeans. I couldn't continue to wear them under my clothes. It was too hot. And I couldn't risk leaving them in the house. If time were to flip, I'd have to return with the garments I wore.

Then I looked at the armoire again. Off to the side were small purses. Handbags. They looked as if they were sewn from tapestry with all sorts of designs. I selected the largest one and stuffed my jeans into it, cinching it up with the blue ribbon that closed the bag.

Just as I started to put on my shoes, I heard a quick knock at the door. I had to say something.

Oui?

"It's me Aeden. We need to talk before anyone else gets up."

Ryn had the same idea I did. He was already dressed but had to cover his jeans with trousers. And, he had managed to stuff his sneakers into the sleeves of one of those really frilly jackets that men wore. Guess his armoires had lots of shoes, too. I walked toward the window and spoke softly.

"I wanted to see you last night, Ryn, but I couldn't."

"No kidding. I don't know about you but I felt like Little Lord Fauntleroy, what with the fancy food, not that I'm complaining, but the bath thing. Jeez! There was no way, no darn way I was going to let Simeon wash any part of me in that tub!"

"I know what you mean. But Renard and Anjenet must be used to it, wherever they are."

"That's another thing. We'd better hope they're safe and sound in Normandy."

"So now what do we do? I heard *Chastain* and *Bastille* in the same sentence so I'm figuring that our great, great relative is locked up. Am I right?"

"Yeah, Aeden. You're right. We just have to find a way to see him. He's not safe."

"Are you crazy? They'll probably bring us to the nearest guillotine if we try to see him."

By now I had walked over to the dresser that held the small collection of dolls. I reached my hand out and touched one of the porcelain dolls gingerly as Ryn grabbed my arm and stopped me.

"Don't get too comfortable here, Aeden. Fancy clothes. Delicious food. And now you're what? About to play with dolls when we need to warn Monsieur Chastain? You are not Anjenet. And we have business to take care of. Now."

I've got to admit, there was a small part of me that wanted to stay in that gilded room. The room with the dolls, the clothes, the soft bed and the window that overlooked the garden. But then I remembered the look Lizette had given me and I even remember what she said.

"Ryn, what does *'Votre secret est bien garde. Je ne vais pas le diré'* mean?"

"Why? Who said that?"

"Lizette. She said it last night when she tried to help me bathe."

"It means we've been found out, Aeden. It means we need to move fast."

Chapter Twenty-Three: Ryn

I saw the way Aeden looked at those dolls and lightly touched their clothing. And she had combed her hair using those bitty little combs to hold it in place. Yeah, she was getting too cozy here, even though we had just arrived the night before. And now she tells me that her servant knows the truth. I knew we couldn't pull off this charade much longer. And besides, we had to see Monsieur Chastain. Before she could say another word, I grabbed her by the arm and headed for the main stairway.

"We've got to find the housekeeper. Right now!"

I could smell freshly baked bread and something wonderful cooking in the kitchen as we got to the foot of the stairs. Aeden was beside herself.

"Can't we just have breakfast first? We never know when or where our next meal is coming from. And I'm not going hungry, Ryn."

"Shh, someone's coming."

Simeon appeared from the dining room and motioned for us to sit down. He apologized for not being in my room to assist me with dressing but thought I would be sleeping longer. Then, he raced into the kitchen, but not before motioning us to sit down at the table.

The kitchen staff had just started to put out large platters of food—breads, cheeses, warm butter, and hot crepes filled with cheeses and jellies. Aeden and I were each given our own teakettle.

"Okay, maybe you're right. We should eat something," I whispered as I picked up a fork and dove into the crepe.

More platters arrived. Spicy meats and fish in varying sauces. I was about to take a stab at one of the meats when Aeden gave me a slight kick under the table.

"Slow down. You're eating like a barbarian. Anjenet and Renaud were probably taught really fancy table manners."

I hated to admit it, but yeah, if I was going to be Renaud, then I needed to act a bit more refined.

In the presence of the servants and wait staff, I pulled off my greatest acting feat—pretending to have decent table manners.

When we finished eating, I told Simeon that it was imperative I speak with the head of the household staff. He left the room, only to return with the same housekeeper who had greeted us the night before and it looked as if she had been crying all night.

"Oh my poor dear Renaud. They've taken your father to the Bastille. Arrested for treason. Treason. Can you imagine a worse fate? And what will become of you now? You and Anjenet were supposed to be safe with friends in Normandy. Monsieur Chastain is no more guilty of treason than that statue on the wall. I fear for his life."

I reached out and held her hands. Renaud would have done that, I think. And it was convincing, even for my sister, who by now was aching to know what was being said.

"Madame, Anjenet and I must be taken to see our father. He is a prisoner, but prisoners have rights, no? And he can have visitors. I know this."

Truth of the matter was that I had no clue. But I did remember reading *A Tale of Two Cities* and they allowed that guy in the garret to have visitors. So what if it was fiction? It was all

I had. The housekeeper gave me a hug and continued to speak.

"I can arrange for the carriage to take you, but I warn you, it will be a dreadful experience and I am not sure Anjenet will have the...the composure to handle it. The Bastille is enormous. Who knows the conditions under which your father is forced to live?"

"No matter. We must see him at once. Please make the arrangements."

"Oh my sweet Renaud. I have held you and your sister since you were babies and your mother passed away. I could not bear to see any harm come to you. I will send for the carriage at once. And I shall send your father some warm croissants and cheeses. Take care. Take the utmost care."

Then she left the room, leaving Aeden and I to finish eating, but after that conversation, I wasn't too hungry.

The carriage did arrive and it looked like something out of Cinderella—white with gold trim and fancy wheels. The driver was dressed as if we were on the way to a royal ball and not to the most notorious prison in history. Two black horses stood at attention while Aeden and I were escorted into the cab. I remembered the last time I had been taken anywhere on a horse and I shuddered. At least this time, I didn't have to sit on the darn animal.

In daylight we could see just how affluent our neighborhood was. Large fancy houses, beautiful gardens, and servants cleaning steps, trimming bushes, and polishing doorknobs. We headed down Rue Da Guerre to a large boulevard, and that's when things began to change. No more servants tidying the houses, just a large street with big buildings, more carriages and people everywhere. And none of them, it seemed, were too interested in cleaning. But then it started. The odor. The stinking, rotting odor. Not as bad as the sewer, but not a whole lot better. Even the horses made weird noises as we moved along the street. I elbowed Aeden and made a face.

"My God, the whole city seems to stink."

"And it's getting worse. So crowded. Sounds like everyone's yelling at once."

"Yeah, but take a good look Aeden, they're trying to sell stuff. The place is filled with vendors. At least we know one thing—the revolution hasn't started yet. They're still shopping!"

"What the heck? Did you just see that? Someone threw a bunch of straw down on the street!"

"Look ahead. More people are throwing straw, but I don't think it's to feed the animals. I don't get it."

"Can you understand what anyone's saying?"

"Yeah, they're selling stuff—lanterns, shell fish, brooms and animal skins. At least that's what I could make out."

"It's really starting to reek here and the street's getting narrower."

"Nah, it only seems that way 'cause it's getting more crowded."

Aeden tried to cover her mouth but the stench was really gross. Worse than the urinal at camp. I felt like gagging, too. Then, after what seemed like hours, we were on a small bridge over the Seine. River smell. Not much better, especially if all that crap gets dumped in here.

Another tight street with more vendors and large buildings. I could see laundry hanging from poles that extended out of the top windows from the apartments.

"How much longer do you think?" Aeden asked as she pulled her purse closer to her chest.

I shrugged as I glanced at three or four filthy little kids fighting in the street. The people around them didn't seem to care.

Aeden continued to speak.

"Do you have a plan once we get there?"

"Again with the plans? No, Aeden. I don't have an exact plan. The only plan I have is to do whatever it takes so that Monsieur Chastain stays alive. And we've got to start by warning him."

"Big help that's going to be. I don't think he needs to be worried about someone cutting his throat, Ryn, when the biggest knife of all is attached to a box and a pulley! He's already figured out that he's in trouble."

"Then maybe we need to find a way to get him out of there."

"GET HIM OUT OF THERE? WE'LL BE THE ONES DRAGGED TO THE GUILLOTINE!"

"Keep your voice down. Someone might hear you."

"I don't know how. It's crazy loud in these streets. See for yourself. It's like people are getting all stirred up out there. And I mean it, Ryn. We can't do anything stupid."

"Not stupid, Aeden. Just necessary."

Then, for no reason at all, she kicked me and started to cry. I swear, she'd become unbearable.

Chapter Twenty-Four:
Aeden:

Maybe Ryn didn't feel it, but I was certain the atmosphere outside was starting to change. The people on these streets weren't buying and selling stuff. They seemed to be arguing and gathering in small groups. I felt relieved when the street widened and there was just a large stone wall separating it from the enormous building in front of us.

It took me a few seconds to grasp what I was seeing—eight huge towers connecting a frightening fortress. La Bastille. La Bastille Prison. As we entered the first wall I could see soldiers gathering stones and other objects and placing them against the wall, just waiting to volley them onto the other side. But there was no one on the other side. Not now anyway. Still, the soldiers were preparing.

Our carriage passed over a small drawbridge that led to another courtyard. Here, we were greeted by two guards. Our driver stepped down from his seat and handed the guard something. A piece of paper. Rolled and tied with a gold ribbon. Ryn held a finger to his lips and whispered.

"I think that's permission for us to enter. Don't make a sound."

I couldn't understand what the guard and driver were saying, but the next thing I knew, the driver opened the door to our compartment and the guard looked at our faces. No reaction when he stared at me, but the moment he laid eyes on my brother, he turned to the driver and said "*Chastain.*" Then he motioned us forward.

The horses moved slowly as if they wanted to be somewhere else. Anywhere else. Then we stopped under a small archway. The driver opened our door again, reaching out his gloved hand to help me down the small step on the side of the carriage. But instead of helping Ryn, he leaned in and spoke. A language that still mystified me, but a tone I recognized.

"You and your sister have been granted permission to see your father, but I warn you, it's dangerous. You can still change your mind. I will give the horses water and rest at the stables nearby and shall return for you before

dusk. We should not be traveling on the city streets at dark."

Then Ryn spoke.

"Do not wait for us. Give the horses water and rest, then leave at once. The servants in our household will be safe as long as the Chastain family is not present. Do not argue. You must do as I say."

"But Monsieur... I implore you. Do not stay in this place."

"I have no intention of staying. Now go. Quickly."

The driver helped Ryn out of the cab and immediately took his place at the helm, grabbing the reigns and turning the carriage back so that it faced the small drawbridge. Then, he leaned down and handed Ryn the piece of paper. I recognized the next words he said but had no idea how much they would mean to us in the next few hours.

Bonne Chance!

I didn't need to speak French in order to understand what my brother had done. The words flew out of my mouth like cinders leaving a fire.

"Why did you get rid of our carriage? What's the matter with you? Now we'll never get out!"

"Take a look at the notice that's posted by the wall, Aeden. It's a large enough sign. And even you can figure it out."

I looked at the piece of parchment someone had attached to the guard post. It was a calendar, indicating the day, month and year. And that's when I knew that something was about to go terribly wrong.

LUNDI, JULLIET 13, 1789

"Stop staring at the notice, Aeden. We've got to walk over to the guards and hand them the paper."

I felt numb, waiting for the words to sink in. *LUNDI, JULLIET 13*. I already knew the year. My feet moved automatically. I was blotting out everything around me. That's why I didn't hear the commotion at first. Ryn had to yank me to the side so two soldiers could escort a prisoner forward. They walked directly past us, the prisoner shouting all sorts of tirades. Then he turned his head around and looked me straight in the eye. I tried to control my reaction but I wasn't sure that I had managed to do so. It happened way too fast.

"Michel," I started to scream as my brother put his hand over my mouth. Wasting no time, I jabbed Ryn in the side and ran toward Michel, who looked at me as if I had committed the worst betrayal.

"What's this? The little sewer rats dressed in finery? I do not understand."

Ryn was directly behind me and tried to respond but it was too late. One of the soldiers lashed out at Michel with a slap to the mouth. I couldn't help myself. I screamed out one of the few words I knew.

"NON!"

Then the soldier turned toward me. The words were incomprehensible but the intent was frightening.

"You know this man?"

Ryn immediately spoke.

"My sister is mistaken. She thought it was someone we knew. But clearly, that is impossible."

The soldier never moved. He just looked at Michel and then at us. Then he started to laugh as he waved us toward the guards. I bit my lip as I watch Michel put his hand to the bruise on his face.

"Pardonnez moi," I mumbled. Again, an expression I had heard somewhere.

The soldiers dragged Michel past us. I watched, horrified, as they threw him down to the ground in front of a small door by one of the towers. As one of the soldiers opened the door, I could hear Michel yell. And his words were meant for us. Words that I had once uttered a long time ago on my first flight to Paris.

"Gorges de certaines personnes méritent d'être coupé, vous le savez."

But what people deserve to have their throats cut?

PART TWO:

LA BASTILLE

Chapter Twenty-Five: *Ryn*

I'd heard of heart palpitations and now I had them. Right in the middle of the Bastille courtyard. I swear, my sister was going to get us either killed or locked away in some dark cell. That's all we needed. For the soldiers and guards to think we were in cahoots with some guy who was part of a clandestine secret society. I mean, it wasn't as if I didn't want to help Michel... After all, he did save Aeden from falling into the sewer. But here? In the middle of the Bastille? One wrong move and we'd all be arrested. Aeden had to get it into her head that she was Anjenet and I was Renaud. That simple. If we dropped our false identities we'd be dead meat. I reached for her wrist and mouthed the words, *"Are you nuts?"* Okay, so I could have said something a bit more reassuring, but frankly, I was getting really tired of her emotional outbursts.

We walked directly to the two guards who were positioned across from the courtyard gate, glancing only once at the tower to our left that now held Michel. Our pace quickened as we got closer to the guards. Without wasting a moment, I held the letter directly out in front of me. One of the men snatched it from my hand, without even bothering to look at me. Then he proceeded to read it as if he were my father reviewing one of my report cards, only this guy wasn't concerned about tardiness or goofing in the hallways. Then, he waved the letter in front of the other guard before he spoke.

"So... you are the Chastain children, here to visit your father."

"Oui, Messieurs," I responded, without moving an inch from where I stood.

"You will be taken to his quarters, but you cannot stay long. This is not some countryside visit with the amenities you privileged ones are accustomed to receiving."

"I understand. We just wish to see our father."

I expected the worst. A cold, dark cell in some rat infested dungeon came immediately to mind. And even though Aeden and I had maneuvered the sewers and managed to crawl through the catacombs, we were in no way prepared for what we were about to see.

One of the guards led us to the tower on the opposite side of the one where Michel was being held. It was a massive spire of brick that seemed intimidating the minute we set foot inside. Small oil lamps lit a circular staircase. *Again, circular stairs. It was as if the French couldn't figure out how to build a damn staircase without getting all of us dizzy.* I expected to be climbing downstairs so I took my first step down before the guard spoke.

"Where are you going? Your father's room is upstairs. This way. Follow me."

Aeden and I held the railing as we climbed up the stone stairs. She slowed down for just a second to touch something on the wall, but since she didn't scream or anything, I figured it was okay to keep moving. I could see wooden doors at each level. All of them closed and bolted from the outside. My stomach started to churn as I remembered all of the classic French prisoners who were never to see the light of day. *The Man with the Iron Mask, Voltaire, Marquis de Sade— okay, so maybe he deserved it, but still...* I wondered who they had housed behind these doors but decided not to ask. Aeden would occasionally let out a small cough or sigh as we kept walking. At least I knew she was behind me.

We stopped after three or four flights. The guard unbolted a door and then proceeded to open another lock, just above the doorknob. I expected to be ushered into complete darkness but the light from the windows in the room allowed us to see everything in complete detail and that's when Aeden let out a gasp that took us all by surprise. While I was intent on looking at the room, my sister caught sight of Monsieur Chastain, who was seated at a desk near one of the large windows. As he stood up, I could see why Aeden almost lost it. Monsieur Chastain was me. Me, twenty or so years from now. For a split second, I imagined the worst. Were we going to be stuck here in 1789 and Monsieur Chastain was really me? But then, I remembered some law of nature. Newton, maybe? *No two objects can occupy the same place at the same time.* I started to relax. We just looked alike, that's all. Family resemblance. I was, after all, a Chastain, just not *this* Chastain.

My mind was doing a hundred things at once—looking at the room and realizing that it was as close to a fancy hotel as anything I could have imagined, wondering what to say to Monsieur Chastain, hoping Aeden wasn't going to start crying or doing anything idiotic, and wondering how the hell we were going to get out of here. If I felt dazed, I must have looked it, too, because Monsieur Chastain was certain that I was Renaud and that something horrendous had happened.

The guard had closed the door behind us and I could hear him bolt the lock, but all I could do was stare at Monsieur Chastain until he finally spoke.

"Renaud, Anjenet, what are you doing here? What has happened? You were supposed to be on your way to Normandy. This is a disaster. It is much too dangerous for you to remain in Paris. Please, what has happened?"

In an instant, I had to decide if Aeden and I were going to pretend to be his children or just tell him...what? That we came from another century? That we had to get him out of the Bastille before morning? That one of the biggest revolutions in the world was about to start? He would think we had gone mad. Lunatics. Lunatics who belonged in the dungeons. I had to think of another way to broach the subject but the words wouldn't form in my mouth. Again, he spoke.

"Whatever has happened, I must know. The guard will be back for you soon. I must find a way to help you."

Then, somehow, my courage returned and I answered him.

"Actually, we have come here to help you, father."

Chapter Twenty-Six:
Aeden

The building engulfed me like a giant accordion that was about to crush me into one of its folds. I'd never seen anything so massive. Two courtyards and eight towers. It was almost incomprehensible to think that we could possibly change anything, let alone save Monsieur Chastain. The only thing I understood with any amount of certainty was the date. We were one day away from the throng of humanity that would ultimately take down this prison. Hundreds of people, thousands of people... We'd be trampled and stomped on, thrown under whatever human siege was about to happen. We'd die under the grinding anger that festered for years in this place. I was stunned. And just as I was beginning to make sense of the date and time that were posted in the courtyard, I saw Michel.

Michel, who had reached down and pulled me up before I got swept into the sewers... Michel, who thought we were like him – intent on wielding a knife across someone's neck just as easily as he had drawn a line across their names on his wall. I was numb, and too overwhelmed for fear. There just wasn't time.

Monsieur Chastain raced towards us and embraced us in his arms. I had no idea what he was saying and tried to think of anything that I could say in French that would make sense under these circumstances. Then, I remembered an old movie I once saw. A love story. And I remembered what they kept saying. So I said it, too.

"Je t'aime."

The man rustled my hair and gave me a hug. Then he motioned for my brother and me to be seated on a decorative couch near one of the windows. He carried the wooden chair that was by the desk and placed it directly in front of the couch. As he took a seat, I knew instinctively that he was about to tell us something important. I pretended to absorb every word but kept an eye on my brother to see his reaction. It was the only barometer I had.

Monsieur Chastain cleared his throat and spoke quietly.

"My dearest children, you must have suffered some awful fate or you would not be here today. It is my fault entirely. In trying to save you, I may have placed you in the very danger I was trying to avoid. Paris is no longer safe for those of us in the aristocracy. A growing turmoil will consume us. I did not want to frighten you with the details. But the details tell it all. One by one, members of the aristocracy are being murdered. Their throats cut. One slash across the neck and then three small cuts, symbolizing the Fleur-de-lis. Many have succumbed to this insane violence. That is why I had you sent to Normandy and created a pretense for my 'arrest.'"

"You mean you did not commit treason?" Ryn asked.

"Of course not. I would no more commit treason than steal from my own mother. It was all a pretense. A carefully arranged pretense so that I would be unharmed in the Bastille until this fury was over. Until it was safe for me to return home and..."

Before Monsieur Chastain could finish the sentence, Ryn broke in.

"It will never be safe for you to return home. That is why we have come here. Anjenet and I have seen too much unrest in the streets. A revolt is about to take place, Father. We

have heard people talk. They are planning to storm this very prison. We must find a way to escape immediately."

Monsieur Chastain reached forward and gave my brother's hand a pat. The kind of thing adults do when they want to tell you that everything's going to be okay.

"Fear not. Didn't you see the amount of ammunition that the soldiers have stored by the walls? We are safe. The Bastille is impenetrable."

Then Ryn got really loud.

"No, it's not. I mean... well, with all the fighting, someone is bound to get in and none of the prisoners will be safe. Not even you."

At that instant there was a quick rap at the door and the sound of someone unlocking the bolt. I started to get up but Monsieur Chastain motioned for me to remain seated. He walked toward the door as if his countenance alone would be able to save us from any impending doom. Then, I heard three words and they didn't sound the least bit frightening.

"Votre repas, Monsieur."

Someone was bringing Monsieur Chastain his dinner. I felt the color return to my face. A haggard looking woman stepped inside the room and placed a large covered tray onto a table that faced the rear part of the room. I never found out what that dinner was. But it didn't matter, because no one was going to eat it.

I don't know what possessed me. But next to the tray was the large ring of keys that the woman had used to open the door. As she started to lift the cover from the tray, I grabbed the keys and flew out that door knowing full well that Ryn and Monsieur Chastain would be right behind me. Ryn, because he swore he wouldn't let me out of his sight, and Monsieur Chastain, because in the few moments that I had interacted with him, I knew he would do anything and everything to ensure that his children were safe, even if it meant his life.

Chapter Twenty-Seven: Ryn

I never expected it. Aeden taking off with the keys. Charging down the stairs without thinking. I was right behind her, and behind me, Monsieur Chastain. It might have been comical if it weren't for the fact that she was about to get all of us killed. I wasn't so sure what to do either. We couldn't just walk out into the courtyard and risk getting shot by the soldiers. And it wasn't as if that tower had clear passages to the other parts of the Bastille. I wanted to shake Aeden by her shoulders and ask her just what the hell she had in mind, but someone was shouting in my ears and it didn't matter what my sister was thinking. Whoever tried to puncture my eardrums apparently had a plan; and we had no choice but to follow it.

"To the kitchen! Go to the kitchen. Now!"

The woman who had brought the food tray to the room was directing us to the kitchen.

"Where?" I yelled. *"How?"*

"Keep moving down the stairs. Don't stop at ground level. Two more flights down. A large archway and then a long passage. Keep moving."

I caught up with Aeden before we even got to the floor below us. It was no time for pleasantries. I grabbed her shirt by the shoulder, leaned it and whispered.

"We're headed for the kitchen. All the way down."

What I really wanted to say was, "We're headed for the kitchen, unless of course you have other plans and would care to stop and share them with us." But there was no time for sarcasm and no time to stop and talk. I knew Aeden would just keep moving, and she did.

When we got to the passageway that led to the kitchen, it was wide enough for me to walk next to her, even though there was nothing I could say to her at this point, and frankly, if there was, she wouldn't want to hear it.

"This is it," the woman exclaimed as we approached the archway. *"If you go through the kitchen, it will take you to a series of tunnels and passages. Each tower is connected to a tunnel. Good Luck!"*

"Give her back the keys, Aeden," I mouthed, hoping that she'd be able to read my lips in the dim oil lamp light of the kitchen.

Aeden understood. She walked toward the woman and extended the keys.

"No, you'll need these more than I, little girl. Hurry."

Then the woman pushed the keys back into Aeden's palm and said something to Monsieur Chastain. I could tell that whatever it was she had told him, made him realize that I was right and that we had to escape.

In less than 18 hours a vicious mob of angry citizens was about to break through and I had no intention of offering them my head for a quick decapitation. We didn't have many options. Actually, we didn't have any, except for one—the sewers under the Bastille. I tried not to think of the filth and the stench, but hey, what else do you think of when you're dealing with sewers? If this were one of those balance scales, it would be a no brainer. Crazed angry people with guns and knives on one side or sticky smelling watery crap on the other. I'll take the crap. But I was in no position to take anything. I had no idea how to maneuver our way through that maze and the only person who could help us was probably cuffed to the wall of a dungeon in the tower directly across from ours. Michel. He knew those sewers. He knew the catacombs. Hell, it was probably him right behind us that night and maybe that's how the soldiers got him and arrested him.

Now it was our turn to find him. I reasoned that it shouldn't be that hard. It was, after all, the tower directly across from ours. But now we were in the kitchen, headed down a dark passageway and I had no way of knowing where on earth that tower was. I only knew that if we were going to make it out of here, we needed to get to Michel before anyone else did. Even if it meant tackling an underground labyrinth one corner at a time, until we got it right.

I just hoped we had enough time. The trick is to remember where you've been so you don't waste time taking the same route again. But this wasn't the Hood River Corn Maze back in Oregon. This was some underground rat-maze of a prison designed to keep prisoners from escaping even if someone cuts off their shackles.

I headed straight down the passage, motioning for Aeden and Monsieur Chastain to follow. A large lamp that reeked of oil illuminated more than I had wanted to see. Rats scurrying past us and decaying food and animal droppings all over the place. And this was only a few feet from the kitchen. Guess passing a health inspection wasn't number one on their list. I just hoped Aeden wouldn't get all un-glued and start screaming or crying.

"I know someone who can help us out of here," I said to Monsieur Chastain as we started to head down the tunnel. *"But he's a prisoner in another tower."*

"Down here it is impossible to know one tower from the next. We will just have to follow the passageway until the walls become rounded. Then we'll know that we have reached a tower."

"And then?"

"And then we hope your friend is still alive."

Chapter Twenty-Eight: *Aeden*

The woman shoved the keys back in my hand and pointed to a large passageway just past the kitchen. I watched for my brother's reaction and knew immediately that we were going to follow that long corridor out. At least that's what I was thinking. That the passageway would take us out of here, but I was wrong. It took us deeper into a winding puzzle of walls, doorways, and dead ends. Ryn would whisper to me, from time to time, when he was sure Monsieur Chastain was out of earshot, but it was frustrating and infuriating to listen to people speak and not understand a single word.

I wanted to tell my brother what I had discovered etched into the wall of Monsieur Chastain's tower. One word. One name—*Dampierre*. And I had seen that name before. It was one of the names that Michel had written on his wall the night we first arrived. And then I started to think. There were eight names in all—*Anjou, Artois, Beaulieu, Chastain, Dampierre, Dreux, Richelieu* and *Vermandois*. Why those eight? If Michel's secret society was intent on killing off the aristocracy, then where were the other names? I know for a fact that there were other aristocrats. Families like *Bourbon* and *Valois*. Why weren't their names written on the wall in Michel's room?

It wasn't as if they had been killed already and that's why the names weren't there. These guys wanted to keep track. They wanted to see that thin line cross out a surname so they could feel some sort of snug satisfaction. Then why only eight? In that dark corridor with only my brother and Monsieur Chastain for company, I had lots of time to think about it.

Whatever Ryn and Monsieur Chastain were saying, it made no sense to me. I just kept walking next to my brother with Monsieur Chastain right behind me. I tried to stare straight ahead because I knew that if I were to look anywhere else, I'd see all sorts of vermin and who-knows-what that would give me nightmares for a month. No, I just told myself to look straight ahead. Looking down wasn't going to be an option. Well, not until we had reached the end of the first tunnel.

The light from the torch was a good ways back, and I could barely see the next one on the wall. Still, I kept moving forward. Kept moving until I felt cold, clammy fingers grab my ankle. Then, I reached inside my lungs to let out a scream that would pierce the eardrums of anyone within a ten mile radius. But nothing happened. It was as if fear itself cut my vocal chords like the knife that cut Uncle Henri's throat.

"Aah...ehh...aah..."

It was automatic. I kicked my foot forward, loosening the grip on my ankle and then turned to see what or who had touched me. I must have made enough commotion, because Ryn and Monsieur Chastain starting speaking at once.

"Prisoners."

"Yes, father."

"We must have reached another tower."

Then Ryn pulled me away from the wall and approached it slowly. If I hadn't felt someone's fingers digging into my leg, I never would have seen the cell that was housed into the wall. Only a narrow metal grate separated me from whatever monster was held captive inside. I held my breath as Monsieur Chastain began to speak.

"Who are you? What is your crime? Why are you being held here?"

"I am Edouard Favreau and my only crime was forgery. Not murder, not robbery, not a crime of the flesh, but forgery."

I could see my brother and Monsieur Chastain taking a good look at the cell. Filthy, dirty with nothing but straw on the floor and a small bucket filled with what? Water? Human waste? I tried not to think about it.

"Forgery, you say?" said Monsieur Chastain. *"Then why the need for shackles? I doubt the prison guards have much to fear from a forger."*

I held my keys out to Ryn and that's when I heard Monsieur raise his voice for the first time. And while I didn't understand, I knew enough to step back.

"Non! Do not open that cell. We cannot be sure if that man is who he says. We cannot take the risk."

Then Monsieur Chastain put his arm around me and moved us forward past the arched gateway to the second tower. The man was screaming wildly but we just kept walking. I could see my brother leaning over and whispering something as the man in the cell continued to bellow. But it wasn't until much later when I learned what had been said.

"Forgive me. I cannot help you. But fear not, you will be freed by morning."

"And you, young Monsieur Chastain. Yes, I know who you are. You and your family will rot in hell. I shall see to it myself."

Ryn moved quickly and caught up with us. This time I was intent on looking at everything in the tunnel. I didn't care what disgusting entrails were tossed about. I wasn't going to be taken by surprise again. So I looked carefully. Methodically, with each step I took.

The remaining cells in the base of the second tower were empty. No sign of Michel. Another hallway. Another maze. I just kept walking. But before we left the wider corridor in the tower, I reached my hand to the wall to touch the identical spot where I had felt the etching of the name *Dampierre* in the tower that housed Monsieur Chastain. The letters were carved in the spot at the base of the spiral stairs. The spot where flat stone replaced brick. This time there were fewer letters, but the name was unmistakable —*Anjou*. It was the first name on the list in Michel's room.

Chapter Twenty-Nine:
Ryn

The string of obscenities that Edouard Favreau hurled from his mouth followed us down the tunnel and echoed off the walls. I made a mental note to learn some of them. But I wondered how real his threat was, knowing that he would eventually be set free by a mob of crazed citizens. The thought of it just made me move faster down the hallway and that, apparently, wasn't such a good idea.

"Renaud! Look out! It's a drop-off!"

When I landed face first in a pile of straw and feces, I knew it was a drop-off to a lower part of the tunnel. I wanted to hurl my guts out from the smell. And the smell was now all over me. Crap! Yeah, that was an appropriate word to describe it. And then Aeden started laughing. Laughing! What the hell. If I did that to her, she'd carry on so much that I'd get grounded.

"Merde!" I screamed at her, but Monsieur Chastain replied with *"Yes, we can smell that."*

He lowered Aeden down the three or four foot drop-off. I was still pissed that it had taken me by surprise. *I hate this stinkin' tunnel! And if I ever get my hands on that rotten kid who pushed us in the first place, he'd better watch out!*

Monsieur Chastain jumped down and took the lead as we walked, turning now and again to speak with me.

"It is only a foul odor, Renaud. We must keep moving."

"So you believe me, now. About the situation that is about to happen."

"I thought at first you may have been exaggerating, but the woman who brings my food has worked in this prison for decades. Under her breath, while we were still back in my cell, she told me that the Marquis de Launay, the man who governs the Bastille, was himself expecting a small mob to appear and had told the soldiers to have an arsenal at the walls."

Yeah, if you consider a hundred or so screaming, ranting, weapon wielding zealots a small mob...but I kept my mouth shut. Aeden was a good two or three feet from my side, covering her mouth with her hand as we trudged through what I thought was going to be the lowest part of the prison. It was a miracle that we could even see where we were going. The oil lamps and torch lights were spread far apart, and the tunnel curved so much, that any light at all was dim and smoky.

Aeden seemed to be fixated on the walls of all things, but that probably wasn't so bad considering that she'd spot a doorway or opening into another channel. And then, just as things couldn't get much worse, we hit a dead end. A lousy dead end. Brick wall. Nothing else. Dead end.

"We must have missed something. We'll need to turn back," I said, but Monsieur Chastain didn't agree.

"The channel wouldn't just end. The towers have to connect. We just need to take a closer look."

All I could see in front of me was brick wall. And it looked pretty darn solid. No secret doors, no openings or hidden holes to crawl in, just rock hard solid brick. Monsieur Chastain walked alongside it, touching the bricks carefully until he came to the end of the wall where the tunnel and wall converged. Solid brick. We just stood there, waiting for him to realize that we had no other choice but to turn back.

But the man wouldn't give up. He turned in the opposite direction and walked the wall again. This time, he found what he had been looking for—a way into the next tower.

"Renaud, Anjenet! The wall does not end. It is an illusion. Look here. If you follow it to the other side of the tunnel, you will see that there is a narrow opening. Enough for us to slide through."

I hate narrow openings. Someone always gets stuck. I don't care how much you suck your gut in, someone always gets stuck. And it better not be me. I watched as Monsieur Chastain ran his hand up and down the slit in the wall before taking his first step.

"Once I am on the other side, send Anjenet through."

"Oui," I replied as I motioned for Aeden to get in front of me.

"You must hold your breath. The space is very tight."

Hold my breath. What did he think I was doing all the way through the passageway? My body smelled like the elephant exhibit at the Oregon Zoo. Still, I got the message. The opening was tight.

"Hold your breath," I whispered in Aeden's ear as I pointed to the space in the wall.

She whispered something back and I swear it was a four letter word. I leaned closer so she could catch a good whiff of me. Then I watched as she slid through the opening. My turn. I moved my left arm in first and then followed with my left foot. It wasn't that difficult. I leaned my whole body in and started to wedge forward, but something wasn't right. One of the sneakers that I was carrying got wedged into the opening and I couldn't leave it there. *Why did I ever listen to Aeden about wearing Renaud's shoes and hiding my sneakers? She was insistent that someone would notice. Sure, her toes didn't have to get crammed into her stupid Dr. Martians or whatever you call them. I'll probably wind up with hammer toe, or a bunion. Why do I even bother to listen to her?* Now I had to figure out how to get my sneaker out. I wasn't so much worried about the whole time-space continuum thing, but the fact that I was going to need both sneakers on my feet when we got out of this century, not Renaud's miserable shoes!

"Just a moment," I said. *"My foot is stuck."*

Then, I tried to wiggle my body around so I could get into a decent enough position to pop the sneaker out of its tight spot. I wanted to heave, right there and then. The more I wriggled, the worse it smelled. I swear, as soon as we hit the 21st century, I'm going to set the Guinness Book of World Records for the longest shower ever taken!

Don't ask how I did it, but I did. The sneaker came loose and I tore through that wall with enough force to knock into Aeden, who had managed to add another word to her meager French vocabulary.

"Merde."

Go figure. She knew a curse word.

Chapter Thirty: Aeden

It wasn't my fault that Ryn fell head first into that cesspit, but he acted as if I pushed him or something. Just because I laughed. And it *was* funny. But what happened next scared the living daylights out of me. And nothing could have prepared us for it.

Ryn had barely managed to free himself from the crack in the wall when he came stumbling forward. It was enough momentum to catch me off guard and I fell back, but instead of landing on the floor, I was tumbling head first down steep steps with my brother only inches away, head first. I could feel every scrape, bump and bruise, but the worst part was that I became the cushion for Ryn's landing. The wind was sucked out of me, but I wasn't really hurt.

Softly, so that Monsieur Chastain, who was still at the top of the stairs, would not be able to hear us, Ryn spoke.

"Are you okay?"

"Yeah, just scraped up a bit."

"Those stairs were right on the other side of the wall. What idiot builds something like that?"

"The wall was probably added later, to seal that part off, but they left an opening for the guards or something."

Just then, Monsieur Chastain appeared, reaching his hand to help me up. Ryn was already standing and brushing himself off.

"Anjenet, are you injured?"

"She's all right," Ryn said. *"We both are."*

It took us a few minutes to acclimate to our new surroundings. It was damp, stifling and tight in this lower chamber. The passageway continued but the torch light was so far ahead in the distance that we had to press our hands on the sides of the tunnel to keep us going straight. To make matters worse, there was a sulfurous stench that made me want to gag. Ryn and Monsieur Chastain spoke now and again as I struggled to understand the words.

"Do you think there are any prisoners down here?"

"We would hear them, Renaud, begging for us to open their cells."

As we got closer to the torch light, we started to walk faster. I could see that the opening was getting wider and that we were now inside the bottom of the third tower. But the odor was getting worse. Nauseating. Stomach churning. It was as if someone had left garbage out to rot for weeks and weeks. And then I heard my brother let out a yell.

"My God! Dead bodies. There are dead bodies over there!"

Even I could figure out the word *cadavres*. Dead bodies. He was pointing to a cell that contained bloated, black bodies and that's when I threw up. Monsieur Chastain quickly put his arm around me and gave me a hug.

"It will be all right, Anjenet. All of this will be over soon. Turn your head away!"

Then he put his arm around my brother and spoke.

"Take a good look, Renaud. These are not prisoners. They are soldiers. See the clothing? And look carefully. Some of their weapons are still on the ground. I don't know what happened here, but whatever it was; it took place quite a while ago. Nonetheless, we need to secure those weapons. And I am sure the cell is no longer locked."

I stood absolutely still as I watched Monsieur Chastain pull the cell's metal grate forward and step inside. He waved for Ryn to follow and continued speaking.

"Do not touch their bodies. We do not know what diseases they may now harbor. Just use your legs to kick and see if there are any weapons. And Renaud, do not bother with a musket, we have no ammunition, look for swords or daggers."

If the whole scene weren't so frightening, and the odor so putrefying, it would have been funny. Ryn was leaning back and kicking at the bodies as if he were playing soccer for the first time. Then, I saw him bend down and grab a small, slender dagger. Monsieur Chastain had also found a knife, but his was wider, like something you'd expect to see in a butcher shop.

"Come Renaud and Anjenet, we must get out of this tower."

And while I wasn't exactly sure what Monsieur Chastain had just said, I walked closely behind him as he started down the passageway. Then, I remembered something. Just a hunch, but a strong one. I had to find the spot on this tower wall with the smooth plaque and the writing. And oddly enough, I was beginning to become more confident with the few French words I knew.

"Un moment, s'il vous plaît," I said as I reached my hands to the side walls. First on the left, then on the right. But nothing. That was odd. There should have been a stone plaque with a name on it. Suddenly, it hit me. We were one flight downstairs. Maybe the plaque was on the wall at the top of the staircase. I had to get back up the stairs.

"Un moment, un moment," I uttered as I started up the stairs, hoping Ryn would be able to make some sort of excuse for me. I was tired and my legs felt like Jell-O but I had to see for myself if the name would be on the wall.

Monsieur Chastain ran behind me, but Ryn stopped him, placing the flat palm of his hand on Monsieur's chest. Then, my brother said something that I couldn't quite hear, or understand, for that matter.

"She is not going back. She wants to see something."

I paused for a second to look behind me, but all I could see were two dark figures, standing perfectly still. I kept walking until I reached the top of the stairs. Then, carefully, I moved my fingers across both sides of the walls.

Only five letters, but that was enough. *Dreux*. Another name. Another name from the list on Michel's wall. "This isn't a coincidence any longer," I thought to myself. "But what is it? What does it mean?" But I knew one thing. *Chastain* was also carved into a tower wall, I just didn't know where.

Chapter Thirty-One: Ryn

I just took a dagger off of a dead person. Good thing, too, because now I know what I am *not* going to do for the rest of my life. I can rule out anything in the health profession, anything in the criminal justice system and anything that has to do with the food industry. I just saved some poor guidance counselor a hell of a lot of time.

Aeden had traipsed back up the stairs to check for something. Sure, she didn't have to go near those bodies, so she could humor herself looking for messages on the walls or whatever it was she was after. But I was getting impatient and so was Monsieur Chastain.

"RAPIDE!" I yelled at the top of my lungs, figuring out that she'd understand the word. If it weren't for cognates, half my class would have flunked French.

"Oui," she replied, and I let out a slow breath. I knew she was looking for something, but we had no real way to communicate. I'd just have to wait.

Then, out of nowhere, the walls began to tremble as if something were shaking the fortress apart, brick by brick. Aeden had just made it down the stairs as the second jolt hit.

"Cannons!" I said, not realizing how loud my voice had gotten. *"They're firing cannons to warn any dissidents not to approach the Bastille!"*

Again, another short series of quakes and rumbles, before the building became silent. Monsieur Chastain took my sister's hand, pulled on my sleeve and kept moving as he spoke.

"It is nighttime. And this is just a show of force. No one is approaching. Not at night. This is a warning to stay away. The cannon fire will echo down the narrow streets, delivering the message from the Bastille's governor. But I do not believe that anyone will listen to that message. We must get out while there is still time. Keep moving."

Unlike the vaulted ceilings in the other parts of the passageway, this one was low. So low that I could actually reach up and touch it. I tried not to think about what kind of gross things were dangling inches from my head. My sister and Monsieur Chastain were almost at a jog and I had to take long strides to keep up with them. But this passageway dead-ended, too. Only there was no opening in the brick wall. Just a frayed rope ladder, hanging from a small opening above us. *Damn these people! They couldn't have put in another staircase! I'm not freaking Tarzan!* And even though I didn't say a word, I'm sure Monsieur Chastain could read my mind as he continued to speak.

"Mon Dieu! What imbecile neglected to construct a stairway...unless it was the intent to keep those unfortunates who were housed down here from ever escaping? We are lucky Renaud and Anjenet, for the rope is dangling down. I imagine it is usually pulled up and wound, so that there is no chance of an escape."

I knew what was coming. We were going to have to climb that stinkin' rope. Hell, I couldn't even pull that off in 8th grade during the physical fitness tests. And Aeden? Geez, the closest she ever came to a rope was jumping it! But what about Renaud and Anjenet? Did they know how to climb ropes? Because Monsieur Chastain sure acted as if this was something they did all the time. I felt the saliva gathering in my mouth as he handed me the tip of the rope.

"You will go first, Renaud. Then I will assist your sister and follow closely behind her. When you reach the top, stand still. You don't know what to expect and we need to be cautious."

The rope was coarse and gritty. Probably laden with bacteria and mold. *If the fall doesn't kill me, then the splinters will!* I tried to remember how to do this. Something about a quick jump and tucking my legs around each other. But I was still carrying those sneakers, wrapped up under my arms. Then I had an idea. Aeden could attach them to the rope, along with her bag, once I got up. *If I got up*. Then I'd haul the stuff, send the rope down and see if my sister could manage this feat. *Not as if she had a choice*.

I motioned for her to come over and shoved my sneaks into her stomach, making a tying motion with my hands. *Terrific. Now I'm playing Charades when we're hours away from all hell breaking loose*. But Aeden understood and actually replied, *"Oui, Renaud."*

Then, I grabbed the rope, took a deep breath and jumped, using every bit of strength in my arms to hoist myself up. My legs were wrapped around the coarse twine and they felt every pinch, scrape and tear. *How many feet up was this?* I tried not to think about it and just kept pulling myself up. I could hear Monsieur Chastain shouting, *"Bon Travail, Renaud,"* which was a heck of a lot better than my gym teacher yelling, "Move it, Ryn, we haven't got all day!"

The opening at the top was wider than it appeared from below, and once inside, I could see tall vaulted ceilings and a corridor that was well lit with oil lamps. Aeden secured my sneaks and her bag to the rope and I quickly hauled it up. Then, it was her turn and I had a sinking, crushing feeling. What if she couldn't do this?

I looked down, expecting the worst. But I watched as she tore a piece of material from the clothing we had gotten from Michel and wrapped it around her hands. Then, with a boost from Monsieur Chastain, she started to climb. Slowly at first, then gaining speed. Where had she learned these things? As she got closer to the top, I bent down and grabbed her arms just below the elbows, giving her the final push she needed to climb through the opening. Again, Monsieur Chastain shouted, "*Bon travail de ma fille douce.*"

"What did he say?" Aeden whispered.

"Said you did a good job, shh...."

No wonder the man expected us to know how to climb, because he certainly did. In an instant he shimmied up the rope like a circus performer.

"We don't have much time to talk," Aeden said, leaning into my ear. "But there's something you should know. The towers. They have names. And the names..."

Just then, Monsieur Chastain reached the top of the opening and stood up.

"Quick Renaud, pull the rope up so no one can use it from below."

I did as he said, but it was too late. Whoever may have been on the floor below us was now a few feet away and the footsteps were getting closer.

Chapter Thirty-Two: Aeden

I had just grasped my small bag and Ryn's carefully concealed sneakers when I saw the figure of a stocky man in the hallway perpendicular to ours. Somehow, these corridors were linked together and we were just a few feet from the center point. Whoever was walking had two choices—go straight ahead or veer to the right and meet us dead on. I stood there, mute and powerless, waiting to see what he would do. It was impossible to tell if it was a soldier or a guard, but it didn't matter. They killed first and then sorted things out. I just hoped my brother and Monsieur Chastain wouldn't hesitate to use the stolen daggers.

"Shh... It is all right, children. He has continued walking. We shall wait until he is further down the corridor so he will not see us. Walk quietly. Tip-toe if you must."

We were back on the original floor. At least it appeared that way. The brickwork on the walls mirrored the pattern I saw when we first arrived in Monsieur Chastain's tower. And the hallway was wide with enough torch light so we could gauge where we stepped. Off to the sides were cells. Empty cells. Just straw on the floors. No prisoners. No dead bodies. Just empty cells with metal grating separating them from the hallway. Oddly enough, the locks were still affixed to the doors. Were they expecting to bring more prisoners? And is that where the man was headed?

It felt as if we had been walking for days, not hours, and I was exhausted. My feet stumbled and I felt oddly detached from my body. Still, I knew I wouldn't be able to sleep even if we could take a break.

Ryn had mouthed the word *Michel* to me a while back and I figured that we were looking for him. But would Michel try to kill us if he could? Whatever my brother had planned, I hoped he thought it out. But in my heart, I knew otherwise. "Flying by the seat of your pants" was the way he approached life. And here I was, unable to communicate anything to anyone without risking our lives. I just kept trudging past more cells, more torch lights and more brick walls. And then, I heard a voice. A voice I recognized. But it was in French.

"Over here, my little sewer rats, can you get me out?"

Michel was leaning against the metal grate to a small cell. He looked filthy and his clothing was in shreds. Did they beat him? I had no way of knowing. If I had a key I would have let him out immediately, not pausing for a second to think about his real intentions. But Ryn and Monsieur Chastain weren't as taken. My brother pressed his face against the cold metal and spoke clearly. I tried desperately to latch on to any word that I could possibly understand.

"If we let you out, you must swear on your life that you will not kill us. Do I have your word as a Frenchman?"

"And why should I kill you, my little friend? Or were you lying all along?"

"This is not as it seems. I am…that is, we are….Renaud and Anjenet Chastain. And we must see to it that our father escapes from this fortress before the streets are filled with the blood of our people."

"I doubt the streets will be filling up so quickly with blood. Did you not hear the sound of cannons? Every wall to this fortress is thick with soldiers and weapons. Cannons and

muskets. No one is getting in, or getting out. But I do not wish to rot in this putrid cell much longer. I am sure there are better accommodations in La Bastille." Then, turning his head toward the aristocrat whose name was still scrawled on a garret wall, Michel continued. *"Is this not the case, Monsieur Chastain?"*

"No one is safe in La Bastille any longer. Neither peasant nor aristocrat. I have good reason to believe an angry mob will strike, and when it does, we will all be victims. So....will you help us escape and give your word as my son asked?"

I had heard the expression "palpable silence" before, but now I knew what it was. Michel did not respond, leaving us no choice but to keep walking along the dark corridor. When his cell was no longer visible, Ryn spoke to Monsieur Chastain. I may not know French, but I know the tone and animation my brother uses when he wants to persuade someone to do something. This was no different.

"It is a long story, father. But that man is the only one who can get us out of here safely. And somehow, we must convince him to do so. But there is something you should know. He is part of a secret group... a group of people who use the dagger to slit the throats of aristocrats.

And yet, we have no choice. Time is running out."

"So... he is a Fleur-de-lis. The most driven of all the dissenters."

"If this were any other time or place, his dagger would have already seen our throats."

"And yet, you think you can convince him to help us?"

Ryn put his hand to his throat as if he were shielding it. And then, he said something that I finally understood.

"Oui."

Chapter Thirty-Three:

Ryn:

Okay, so I've got what? Ten minutes to convince some guy not to kill us if we break open his cell. Geez. It's not like I haven't convinced people to give in before, but this isn't like talking ones of my teachers into giving me an extra day to turn in some assignment that was due a week ago, or even getting the "go-ahead" from my father to do some white water rafting on the Rogue River with the guys from my lacrosse team. This was serious stuff. And I had to think fast.

Monsieur Chastain gave me that chance and I didn't want to louse it up. While he and Aeden waited for me at the bend in the passageway, I went back to Michel's cell. And the weird thing was, I could swear Michel knew I was going to come back the entire time. He was still leaning casually on the grating and spoke just as I arrived.

"So, you are willing to take a chance after all?"

"Not exactly. I still need your word that no harm will come to my family."

"You know I am sworn to the Fleur-de-lis, do you not?"

"Yes, and I know that the Chastain name is written on the wall of the garret where you and the others meet."

"So, it would appear that we have little to discuss."

"Perhaps we can reach an agreement."

"I do not understand."

"Look, I shall make it simple. You will die in this cell. Cold. Hungry. Forgotten. No one is coming back. The cells below us are all empty and the soldiers and guards now have other interests. You said so yourself. They are lining the walls of the Bastille, just waiting to fire off cannons and muskets at the mob they expect. Do you really think someone is going to take the time to provide food and water for you? You are dead already. It is your choice."

Yeah, I used his own argument back at him. *You said so yourself.* That always seems to work. I just stood still and waited for a response.

"What are the terms of the agreement?"

Holy cow! Terms of the agreement? I felt as if I were back in some boring history class and was just told to recite the terms of the agreement that ended World War I. What was it? Something French, too. Oh yeah, the Treaty of Versailles. My mind was getting jumbled and I had to concentrate.

"In exchange for letting you out of this cell, you will agree not to harm my father, my sister or me. And to ensure that other members of the Fleur-de-lis do not harm us either. In addition, you will show us the way out of here."

Michel stood there, quietly and I stared at him without as much as moving a muscle on my face. The absolute silence in the hallway seemed to stretch out every second. We were at a stand-still and I wasn't about to budge. Then, he finally spoke.

"There is no honor in rotting away in a fetid cell. So, my little sewer rat, I will agree to your conditions. You, your sister and your father shall be safe from my hand or any that wish to use the dagger. But remember, the Fleur-de-lis will have progeny, too."

Was he threatening future generations? What the hell! I can't be responsible for everyone. And we don't have time to write a first draft, make revisions, proof read it and fine tune it. This wasn't my English class!

I let out a sigh and shook my head.

"Agreed. Now let's work on that lock."

"One more thing, my friend," Michel said as I turned to get Aeden and Monsieur Chastain. *"What makes you think that I know a way out of here?"*

"Because, this is not your first time in La Bastille."

"Touche!"

Chapter Thirty-Four: Aeden

"*Les cles!*" Ryn demanded as he held open his hand. I turned the keys over to him quickly and followed him back down the hallway. Monsieur Chastain was right beside me.

"So you believe this man will show us the way out and not devise a means to slice our throats?"

"Yes, father, I do."

The large metal ring held at least twelve keys and I knew the cell wouldn't open on the first try. But Michel kept pointing to the ring itself and repeating the word *lettre R. Lettre R.* Letter R! Even I could figure it out. The key chain was marked and a key with the letter R would open his cell.

Ryn immediately found the long skeleton key that had a deep impression of the letter R on it. The lock came open on the first try and Michel stepped into the corridor. My brother shook the key ring in front of Michel's face and spoke.

"How did you know that the key to your cell was marked with the letter R?"

"Mon Dieu. Don't you know? I've had the luxury of staying in this delightfully putrid Richelieu Tower."

"Richelieu?"

"Yes, in honor of that fine aristocratic family, the last throats of whom are all marked with the Fleur-de-lis. And now it is my turn. Whose neck did you cut to secure that ring of keys?"

Ryn gave me a funny look, as if he were going to ask me something but then realized he couldn't.

"Let's just say we happened upon some good luck."

"Well, we shall all need it, in order to escape. There is only one way out of this fortress for us. The walls are heavily guarded and the soldiers are poised to shoot. Any exit on land will be an invitation to a swift death."

"So," Monsieur Chastain said, *"if I understand you correctly, the way out will be underground."*

"Yes, underground and under water. And we cannot try it at night. In pitch black darkness even the best sewer rat will become confused. We must wait till morning and I know the perfect hiding place—the central tower that housed only the finest of guests. I doubt it is occupied. But there is access to water and chamber pots. But getting there is another matter. It is sealed off from the other towers."

"What do you mean?"

Michel spoke directly to Monsieur Chastain, turning his head only once or twice to acknowledge Ryn and me.

"There is a large moat at the end of the passageway. Had you not stopped to free me, why, you might have all fallen in. They keep it deliberately dark. Entrance to the central tower is outside the building. In another century, there was a small drawbridge above the moat. But that was another time and the bridge is long gone."

I could see that my brother was becoming edgy and impatient. Even the tone of his voice was strained.

"So, how do you propose we cross the moat?"

"From above and I do hope you are not afraid of heights or rats."

"We have already climbed on ropes and seen rats in this place."

"The rats should not be a concern. They just startle you and go about their business. But, my friend, there are no ropes. We must climb with our hands on the edges of the brick. Then, at the top, where the archway crisscrosses, we can grasp the wooden planks and with enough force, propel ourselves over the moat."

"Propel ourselves?" I heard Ryn gasp. *"Propel ourselves?"*

"Yes, unless you wish to be consumed by the waste from the Bastille's garderobes. All of the Bastille's sewage sluices into the moat."

"Are there any other choices?"

"Why of course, my little friend. You can have your choice of any of the guns or cannons that will be aimed at our heads."

Monsieur Chastain gave my hand a squeeze and said something. It didn't matter what. I knew we were in trouble.

Chapter Thirty-Five: Ryn

A moat filled with sewage. Yep, the day couldn't get any worse. But at least we had a guide who knew this place and could get us out. None of us said a word as Michel took the lead and headed down the passageway. More empty cells. More foul odors from the dampness and decay. Then, it dawned on me. The odor was coming from me. I was just as gross as anything down here. A regular advertisement for 18th century sanitation. I just hoped I wasn't harboring some skin-eating, bone gnawing disease on my body. And the more I thought about it, the more I began to itch.

It seemed as if the corridor out of this tower would never end. I started scratching the back of my neck and my arms. Maybe a good swim in the moat would kill off anything growing on me... I was so busy thinking about what godforsaken things were taking hold of my body, that I didn't notice how much darker the passageway was getting until the only light seemed to be so far in the distance that the floor and walls were no longer visible. I started to walk slower.

"So you have noticed it, too," Michel said. *"This is the last of the light for this tower. That's why the moat is so dangerous. It takes you unexpectedly. Walk very slowly. There will be enough light from the adjoining tower to let us cross."*

Oh, great. Crossing a moat in the dark. Just what I always envisioned. Who needs dirt biking, skateboarding or surfing when you can cross a stinkin' cesspit of a moat in a fortress that's about to be stormed? I let out a slow breath and kept walking. Monsieur Chastain was whispering words of encouragement to Aeden but she didn't reply. I mean, after all, how long can you keep saying *oui* or naming various foods?

Michel stopped suddenly and stretched his arms out to prevent any of us from walking.

"Take the smallest of steps and put your foot down slowly, feeling for ground."

I knew Aeden would be okay since Monsieur Chastain was right next to her. But could she make the climb once we got to the moat? Then again, she surprised me before when she managed to wriggle up that rope. But this was scaling a wall. Even rock climbers use carabiners or pitons. And the ones who don't want to mar the environment use special gloves and special shoes. Crap! We have nothing!

Monsieur Chastain and Aeden stood still as Michel kept edging forward. He was right. In the distance was a dim light. A dim light in another tower. We had reached the moat.

"Look for the jutting edges on the bricks and use them. Hoist yourself up until you can reach the wooden planks. Then, lean forward and push off from the wall. Watch!"

Michel made it sound easy. Just like my Phys Ed teacher whenever we had to learn something new. *Well I've got news for you, buddy! This isn't a lousy lesson and I don't care if I get a D! I just don't want to land in crap. I've had it with crap!* Just then, Aeden pushes her way in front of me and starts for the wall, shoving her bag at me. The sneakers and the bag wouldn't be a problem. I'd throw them across the moat. The problem was that my sister, who never managed to get a decent grade in any Phys Ed class, was now scaling a wall that scared the living hell out of me. And no one would be able to catch her if she fell.

Unlike the night at the Beaulieu mansion, she didn't need Michel to hoist her up. At times she wedged her shoes into the open spots of the wall where the brick had crumbled. If she couldn't find an open spot, she stretched out a leg and used the tip of a jutting brick. Monsieur Chastain and Michel were both giving her advice as to where to step and how far left or right she should be climbing, but they might as well have recited the Declaration of Independence for all she knew. As for me, I was flabbergasted. I never expected my sister to pull off a stunt like this. Not without my help, anyway. And this time I was no help. I was just another spectator.

When Aeden reached the top, I could tell she was trying to figure out her next move. Michel was giving her directions, step by step, but it was no use. She had to figure it out on her own.

"Take your right foot off of the brick, turn your body and stretch your right hand so it reaches the wooden plank. Lean your weight back so you pivot around. Then you can place your right foot on another brick, but you will be facing forward, not back."

Aeden did none of the above. She kept moving around until she found a large brick that stuck out. It was big enough for both of her toes to fit. Then, she turned quickly and rested her right foot on another brick. Bending her knees and placing her hands behind her back, she leaned forward. I held my breath, expecting a splash of sewage and a litany of curses. None of us dared to move. In the faint lamp light, I watched my sister propel herself forward with some sort of a leap or jump that would be in a category of its own if this were a fitness test.

She landed with both elbows on the hard dirt floor, less than an inch away from the edge of the moat. Monsieur Chastain gasped and walked closer to our side of the murky water. Michel was already scrambling up the wall and shouting something to Aeden.

"I shall be right there. Do not move." It was as if he knew every crevice, brick and mortar hole in the entire structure. We watched him carefully, trying to memorize his every move. In a matter of seconds, he was at Aeden's side, helping her up. I looked at Monsieur Chastain and realized that I needed more instruction if I was ever going to scale this rotten wall.

"You go first. I will be fine."

Monsieur Chastain ruffled my hair and started for the wall. Guess that was how he showed affection to his kids. I don't remember my dad ever ruffling my hair, and if he tried it with Aeden, she'd throw a fit. But in way, it was kind of nice.

Again, I watched the process. *Dig your feet into the little crevices, use the jutting brick, maneuver yourself around, and then take a leap into mid-air. Yeah, like that was going to happen*. But it did, and Monsieur Chastain landed safely. Now it was up to me. I eyeballed the wall and the moat, taking a deep breath. Then, I made a decision. I was not going to climb it.

Chapter Thirty-Six: Aeden

I knew Ryn wasn't going to climb that wall. But watching him turn the other way and run down the passageway really freaked me out. And it must have done something to Michel and Monsieur Chastain because they were both yelling at him. Yelling at someone who was running in the opposite direction. I kept straining my eyes to see what he was doing, but it was no use.

Michel was about to climb back and get him when all of a sudden we heard a "whooshing" sound. Ryn was tearing down that passageway, coming straight at us, as if he were chasing after a ball in lacrosse. His feet thundered on the dirt ground as he charged toward the moat, gaining momentum and adrenaline. I knew what was next, even if they didn't. *He's going to jump. He's actually going to jump!*

I stepped a good distance back from the moat and tugged at Monsieur Chastain to do the same. Michel didn't need an explanation. We stood there, wordless, watching my brother set a new record for an Olympic broad jump, at least twelve feet underground. My mind flashed back to another jump. The one I had to take from a moving train, and in that instant, I knew my brother would make it. He didn't have to land on a moving target.

"Mon Dieu! You could have drowned!" Monsieur Chastain exclaimed as he hugged Ryn.

Michel let out a breath that seemed to convey both relief and agitation.

"Enough with the family sentiments, we must move quickly. A few feet from this moat is a circular stairwell that is embedded in the tower."

"Embedded?" Ryn and Monsieur Chastain said at once.

I knew that whatever Michel was saying had obviously taken everyone by surprise and this was one time I was glad I couldn't speak French.

"Yes, embedded. It is like a ladder that goes around and around, but you cannot see it. The steps are cut into the wall. Just follow them.

And, you can place both feet on one step, before you move to the next."

"Ughhh," I heard my brother utter, but Michel continued to speak.

"Whatever you do, do not look down. It will make you dizzy and you could lose your footing. Just move step by step."

I knew my brother wanted desperately to tell me something but there was no way without revealing who we were, and that was a risk he just wasn't willing to take. Then, I watched his facial movements as he handed me the small bag I had been carrying and I could see him mouth out two words—*"Look up!"*

It was a warning. Whatever we were about to do, would make the climb over the moat look like the kiddie rock wall at the fitness center near our house. I felt the saliva building in my mouth and had to fight the wave of nausea that continued to build in my throat. I had no choice but to tuck the small bag into my shirt. There was no way Ryn could carry that and the sneakers he's been hiding.

At first I couldn't see the stairs, but once my eyes got accustomed to the semi-darkness I could see the pattern of empty spaces on the round tower wall. A straight climb would have been scary enough, but this one meant moving horizontally and vertically in a spiral without losing your focus. I tried not to picture myself plunging head first toward the ground.

Again, Michel took the lead, giving me more time for the fear and anxiety to build inside me like the rage that was about to take over the Paris streets. My hands began to tremble but I listened to what Ryn said. *Look up*. Was that the cure for vertigo? I wasn't sure. This time, Monsieur Chastain wasn't going to take any chances with my brother. He edged Ryn forward so that we wouldn't be subjected to another escapade in the darkness.

I watched as my brother tucked the wrapped sneakers under his arm and started the climb. One foot in the empty space, then the other. He gripped the narrow slots that were above his head, leading horizontally. I bit my lip so hard that I never noticed the blood that had trickled into my mouth until I tasted something metallic. It's one thing to be scared for your own safety and another for someone else's. At least you have some control over your own actions, but the powerlessness I felt at that moment made me forget any concerns I had for myself.

By now, Michel was nearing the top and Ryn was mid-way across. It was my turn. At least I didn't have to jump this time. All I had to do was concentrate. Concentrate and watch my footing. I knew Monsieur Chastain wouldn't take his eyes off of me, but that was little comfort. My movements were slow and deliberate and the climb was tedious and treacherous. I could now see the opposite end of the tower. Ryn was only a few feet away from reaching the top. Michel was already waiting to offer him a hand on the landing.

Then, Monsieur Chastain started his ascent. I could hear him breathing as I moved further up the tower. Only one more full turn on the spiral and I would be at the top. *Please let this be the last climb in this horrid place. And I hate you, Ryn, for this stupid idea. We could be looking at valued art in the Louvre!* My hand reached into one of the empty slots when all of sudden, something crawled out and up my sleeve. A mouse. I could feel it scurrying up my arm toward my neck and in that instant, I let go of the wall.

"AAGHHH!" My scream seemed to echo round and round the tower as if it were coming from the building itself. I was about to lose my grip with the other hand and fall. Every second felt like an hour. The mouse was now on my neck and I was frozen. Paralyzed. *What the heck was the French word for mouse?* My mind flashed every nursery rhyme and children's song that I had ever heard, searching

desperately for that word. What was it? *Le rat?* Then I remembered a movie. A movie with a mouse, or was it a rat? It didn't matter. I screamed as if an army of vermin were attacking.

"RATATOUILLE! RATATOUILLE!"

And then I wasn't at all sure if that was really a word for a small rodent or some sort of recipe. But Ryn knew exactly what I meant and yelled down to Monsieur Chastain.

"I think there's a mouse or a rat on Anjenet! She always says 'Ratatouille' when she's scared."

Next thing I knew, I felt a reassuring hand on my ankle, followed by a light squeeze as if to say, "You'll be all right." The angle of the steps and the circular incline made it impossible for Monsieur Chastain to reach me and pull the mouse off my neck. But somehow, just knowing he was there gave me the courage to reach my hand behind my ear and grab the tiny rodent. I expected to be bitten, but nothing happened. The mouse just stayed in my hand.

My instincts told me to hurl it down to the floor below, but I just couldn't bring myself to kill something for no reason. As creepy as it was, I lifted my top and shoved the mouse into my bag. It wasn't going to hurt me. And then, inch by inch, I continued to move up the steps until I felt Michel's hand grasping my wrist and yanking me forward.

As soon as I could stand, I placed the bag on the floor and watched the mouse run to a dark corner. A dark corner with the faint wording that indicated a new tower – *Vermandois*.

Chapter Thirty-Seven: Ryn

Ratatouille. I can't believe she screamed ratatouille. It's sautéed squash and eggplant for crying out loud! And I know why she did. She thought it meant mouse or rat from some stupid cartoon we watched years ago. First, she gets the word "duck" wrong, now this. I just wish she'd stick to screaming without trying to say anything in French! I had to think fast 'cause no one in their right mind would understand why on earth someone would scream "pan fried squash" when they were dangling from a spiral tower.

But we were upstairs now, away from the dungeon part of the Bastille, in a tower that Michel insisted was reserved for those high level aristocrats whose families had them committed for one reason or another. No straw floors here. It would be just like the room that

Monsieur Chastain was in, only more elegant. At least we'd have a decent place to sleep for a while before we could make our escape in the morning.

A string of oil lamps lit the top of the tower and we could see a few large wooden doors, spaced evenly from one another. Michel walked over to the first door and motioned for Aeden to give him the keys. She glanced quickly at me and then handed Michel the metal ring.

"Stand back, just in case the room is occupied," he said.

I placed my hand on the door and looked right at him before he had a chance to locate the right key.

"What if they're armed? You said these were not ordinary prisoners."

"Do not worry, they have more to fear from us," he replied, moving his thumb across his neck, almost as if he was hoping to stab whoever was inside. Then I began to wonder. Did Michel manage to steal a dagger as well? Maybe from someone in his own cell? A body we hadn't noticed?

Then Michel proceeded to slip the key marked *"V"* into the lock. Monsieur Chastain was blocking Aeden, just in case someone came storming out. But the only thing that came out of the room was the thick odor of perfume. I wanted to gag. I mean, it's not like I haven't smelled that stuff before, but geez, whoever lived there was sure trying to cover up something far worse.

We walked in slowly, taking our time to look around. I suppose if you compared this prison cell to the ones downstairs, it would get a five star review. But, on its own, it stunk worse than anything. Michel was quick to point out that the chamber pots had not been emptied in some time. Now there's an image that's going to give me nightmares well into my twenties!

There was a small bed with some sort of embroidered spread and a few pillows, a desk and straight chair, a larger cushioned chair and one of those couch-lounge things you always see in antique shops. Two large windows, complete with bars, faced the courtyard. A regular Motel 6!

But Michel was right about one thing. There was water. A large porcelain sink that rested on top of a little table had enough water for all of us to drink, or poison ourselves with intestinal parasites, depending upon how you looked at it.

Still, this was our safe refuge for the night. I looked at the courtyard and couldn't see much. A few torches were on the walls below and lots of wooden kegs but no one seemed to be guarding that area. I figured that the soldiers were all lined up by the outside walls, armed and ready for an attack. After all, they had plenty of gunpowder stored in those barrels. Well, they had a long wait. I knew for a fact that the mob scene wasn't going to start until 3:30 p.m. the next day. It was an interesting bit of trivia that stuck in my brain.

Back in 9th grade, when we were first studying the French Revolution, Mademoiselle Claudine said that it began at 3:30 in the afternoon with a screaming crazed crowd. Just then, someone in our class yelled out, "So, it was dismissal time at the Bastille, too?" and everyone started cracking up. That's how I remembered it was 3:30. Dismissal time. We had at least eight or nine hours to rest and prepare for our escape. A long night in a stinkin' perfume laden, chamber pot filled, room with no light. Terrific.

Chapter Thirty-Eight:
Aeden

I knew a woman had occupied this room and I wondered who she was. It was so sad, just the faint odor of her perfume masking the other awful smells. The candle on her desk had burned out, but for how long? I had no idea. Still, there was enough wax for more light. Ryn had the same idea I did because the minute he saw the candle, he grabbed it, went to the hallway and used one of the oil lamp wicks to light it.

Then, we closed the door. I placed the small bag that contained the croissants and cheeses from the Chastain mansion on the desk. It seemed like years ago that their housekeeper had given me the food to take to the Bastille. Well, at least we would have something to eat tonight. Then, I had a really disgusting thought. That mouse was in the bag. I put him there myself. Ugh. What if he bit into some of the food? What if he...? I rationalized that he wasn't in that bag for a long enough time to do any real damage, but how long does it take to spread disease? Still, we were famished. And who knows when or where our next meal would be coming from, if there was a next meal.

My hands untied the bag and I opened it, thankful that it was dark enough in the room so that we wouldn't have to take a good look. There were enough croissants for all of us and ample cheese to spread, even if we had to use our fingers. But I hate the feel of sticky, greasy fingers. I looked around for anything I could use to wipe my hands. And that's when I opened the drawer to the desk.

A small cloth handkerchief was the only thing in the drawer, and just as I was about to wipe my fingers on it, I noticed something. The woman who was held captive here, had used what looked like old coffee grinds to write out a message. And while I couldn't read the language, I certainly could read my mother's maiden name – *Chastain.*

I unfolded the cloth and walked it over to Monsieur Chastain and my brother, who were both seated on the bed. Michel got up from the small lounge to take a look as well. It was a woman's writing, with a flowing, elegant script and words that stung like a scorpion.

"May all the Chastains rot in hell because death is too good for you."

It was signed *"M."* The way the letter M was formed reminded me of something, but I couldn't quite remember what it was.

Ryn could see that I was desperate to find out what was so important that someone had to save bits of coffee grinds to write it. He made a grimace as if to say, "maybe it's just as well that you don't know what was on that cloth tissue." I glanced at it again, this time paying attention to the one word I did recognize from before – *enfer*. It meant hell. And I knew darn well that whatever she had written meant trouble for us. Then I looked at the bottom near the lace edge. Neatly sewn were three initials – M. T. C.

Monsieur Chastain had seen them, too, because he had a ghastly expression on his face that could have meant one thing and one thing only. He knew her.

Taking the handkerchief from my hands, Monsieur Chastain moved his fingers across the initials, took a deep breath and spoke.

"The woman to whom this cloth belonged was Margaux Toussaint Cheverney. I say 'belonged' because I am sure she has died. It is

a tragic story, and as much as it pains me to say, I am part of it.

You see, I was once betrothed to Margaux. Not only was she an aristocrat, but her family was titled. They were the noblesse. And that would have been a good match for the Chastains and Cheverneys. But I did not love her."

Then, looking up at me and gently touching my cheek, he continued. I stood there, wide eyed, wishing that I could absorb what he was saying.

"There was only one woman for me, Renaud and Anjenet, and that was your mother. I broke off the engagement to Margaux, much to the chagrin of my family, never expecting what would come next.

On the night before I was to wed your mother, Margaux snuck into your mother's house and tried to kill her. Fortunately, a servant heard the screams and came running. Margaux had entered the bedroom thinking your mother was asleep and approached the bed with a dagger in her hand. She never got to use it. By the time the servant arrived, your mother had managed to push Margaux to the floor. The dagger slid under the bed. And the rest....Well... others in the household arrived. More servants and your grandparents. No one wanted an arrest. No one wanted a trial and testimony. But something had to be done.

The Cheverneys were contacted immediately. Monsieur Cheverney came to the house himself, late at night with his carriage. He took Margaux directly to the Bastille where she has remained ever since. You see, the nobility can do that, as can the aristocracy. Lock up any member of your family who is unstable and a threat to your title and household. Poor Margaux. She was jilted and angry. And I am to blame for her life sentence within these walls. How uncanny to find ourselves in her room tonight."

I looked down at the embroidered initials on the bottom of the cloth and then glanced at Ryn who was now sitting directly across from me. I was frantic to know who the lady was. When he was sure no one was looking at him, my brother leaned toward me and carefully mouthed out three words—"*Some nut case!*"

Chapter Thirty-Nine:
Ryn

Aeden would have been all teary eyed and weirded out if she really knew the story behind the cloth, so I gave her the condensed version. Now we just had to wait it out until daylight and then follow Michel to the only exit that we could take unnoticed. In spite of being tired, none of us felt much like sleeping and none of us felt safe enough to even try. Personally, I didn't want to get near anything on that bed. The mouse from the tower was probably just the beginning. And bedbugs. This place was probably rife with them. Besides, someone had to keep watch. I stood up, glanced at the darkness outside the window and spoke.

"We should take turns sleeping, just in case. I'll stay awake first and the rest of you can rest."

"It is better if more than one person stays awake. I will keep watch with Renaud," Michel said as he walked toward the door. *"But first, a quick trip to the garderobe. This is a tower reserved for the finest of the aristocracy and it has garderobes on the other side of the narrow doors in the corridor. No chamber pots for me."*

Then he quietly crept out the door. I knew my sister would need to use the garderobe as well, so I explained to Monsieur Chastain that I would walk her there once Michel returned. Besides, it would give me a chance to talk to her, even if it was only for a minute.

So, as soon as Michel stepped back into the room, I stood up, took Aeden by the arm and walked her out the door, the whole time hoping she wouldn't blow it by saying something she shouldn't. And anything she tried to say in French, she probably shouldn't.

The hallway had enough light from the oil lamps for us to see the other doors and once we walked past ours, I whispered.

"There are bathrooms up here. Well, not bathrooms like you'd expect, but wooden planks with a hole in the middle. Last chance Aeden. Go for it!"

"You go first. What if there's vermin in there?"

"Just go. You'll be fine. And hurry up, in case there are still soldiers walking around."

I waited outside the door and then used the room myself. Oddly enough, Boy Scout Camp hadn't progressed much further when it came to outdoor plumbing.

"So what was the handkerchief all about?" Aeden asked quietly.

"It's too long a story. Listen, I don't want to freak you out, but the only safe exit is going to be underground. The sewers. Michel knows them. We can't go outside. If the soldiers don't shoot us, the mob will trample us. Or worse. They went nuts beheading everyone. We've got to make our escape under the Bastille. We'll do it at daybreak before they start storming this place."

"You mean I've got to climb back down some dangerous stairwell or use a rope or...?"

"I don't know what we have to do, Aeden, it's not like a vacation with a tour guide! We just need to follow Michel and make sure Monsieur Chastain doesn't get killed. And I'm sorry about the mouse incident."

"Then why are you laughing?"

"It was pretty funny, actually."

"I could have fallen to my death!"

"But you didn't. Stop being so dramatic. Now hurry up, let's get ba..."

But before I could finish my sentence, we heard pounding coming from one of the doors in the tower. Heavy pounding and someone yelling.

"Will someone open this door! No one has brought me food in days. No one has brought me water. I hear you. Open this door!"

We both froze. Aeden, because she was taken by surprise, and me, because I understood what they were saying. It meant the guards had already deserted this tower. Damn the history books. The revolution was going to start sooner.

Chapter Forty:
Aeden

Whoever was yelling from behind the door sounded desperate. A loud, raspy male voice that reminded me of those old pirate movies. The ring of keys was still in my hand and as I paused in front of the door, Ryn immediately grabbed my wrist as a forceful "*Non*" emanated from his mouth. Then, pulling me away from the door, he spoke.

"Are you crazy? Certifiable? We don't know who's behind that door. People were imprisoned here for all kinds of reasons—your basic government crimes, theft, murder...and oh yeah, don't let me forget the lunatics whose families put them here!"

"But if we don't open that door, he might die in there."

"Or he might get out and kill all of us! Besides, he'll get out soon enough once all hell breaks loose. I only hope we've made our escape by them. Now come on, we've got to get back into the room."

The pounding continued and once we opened our own door, Michel and Monsieur Chastain heard it, too. But apparently, they shared the same opinion Ryn did and refused to unlock that cell.

I sank into the small couch, too exhausted to think about anything. Monsieur Chastain stretched out on the bed while my brother and Michel stared at the window into an empty courtyard. My eyes refused to stay open and I decided to lie down as well. Taking the small bag that had contained the croissants, I started to roll it into a pillow, but something inside the bag stung my finger.

Carefully, with the candle light behind me, and no one looking, I reached in to see what it was. I moved my hand slowly around each crevice that the material had formed. Tucked into a corner was a thin piece of metal and some sort of paper wrapped around it. I pulled the object out as if it were a grenade about to explode in my hand, but when I realized what it was, I let out a sigh of relief. An embroidery needle. A fairly large embroidery needle. Perhaps this bag had been used for someone's sewing.

But what about the paper? Leaning over so that no one could see me, I quickly unrolled it, revealing a message that needed no translation.

"La Bastille est dangereux."
Lizette

Lizette. My servant. Well, Anjenet's servant who knew I wasn't her. Was she trying to protect me? With one hand, I moved the needle to the cloth on my skirt and pushed it through. It would stay just at the tip of my fingers. Just in case. Maybe Lizette knew more than I did. I put my head on the makeshift pillow and tried to ignore the pounding from the next room as I closed my eyes.

It felt as if I had only dozed off for a second or two, but when I opened my eyes, I could see that hazy light, the kind that precedes sunrise, coming in from the windows. Ryn was slumped over on the desk, asleep, while Monsieur Chastain stood by the door and Michel by the window. I closed my eyes again.

Then I heard them talk. Michel first, then Monsieur Chastain.

"Take a good look. Those men are entering the courtyard and they do not appear to be soldiers or guards."

"Someone must have cut the drawbridge down. Still, it's not a huge mob, just a handful of people."

"Wars have started with less. Come on, we must get moving."

Next thing I knew, there was a hand on my shoulder, shaking me awake. Ryn was already standing, moving his arms and stretching.

"Rapide!" Michel yelled. *"Rapide! We must leave this tower at once."*

I took a last look at the perfume laden room where the poor, unfortunate woman had lived. Then, I followed my brother out the door and into the narrow corridor, just past the rounded tower. With Michel in front and Monsieur Chastain behind us, I felt as if Ryn and I were wedged between two bookends. And it was a good thing, because I was scared out of my wits.

Chapter Forty-One:
Ryn

Talk about a lousy night's sleep, I'll never be able to move my neck again, I swear. But at least I didn't wake up with bedbugs. One look out those windows and I knew we were in trouble. Three-thirty, hell! This thing's starting a whole lot sooner. Michel didn't waste any time getting us moving. We had to be out of this tower and into the basement before every sort of low life got cut loose. And we'd managed to make a few enemies on the way, too. Like the screaming guy and that forger from the dungeon. We just had to get to the sewers and find our way out.

"From this tower we can take a crawlspace to the south side of the Bastille," Michel said as he stopped us from walking any further down the corridor. *"There will be a narrow door on the left. It opens to a ceiling channel that*

crisscrosses the Bastille. But it's too dangerous to walk. You must crawl across on your stomach. And do not look down."

Crawlspace was the right word. It was just a narrow plank that spanned a good twenty feet and to make matters worse, there was no light. It would be at least a half hour before the sunlight would even slip through the bricks on the wall. But this time, I wasn't carrying my sneakers. When I used the garderobe, I changed shoes. I mean, who the heck's going to notice? It's dark as hell in here and my sneakers will be covered in all sorts of crap before this thing is over.

I watched as Michel got on his knees and started to move forward. Then I thought of Aeden and prayed to the gods that nothing, not even as much as a flea, would land on her. It was my turn, next. Monsieur Chastain wasn't taking any chances that I'd find an alternate route. One daredevil leap was enough. Besides, this was at least twenty feet and there was no moat underneath it.

Crap! If I can get through this without having a dozen splinters in my fingers it will be a miracle. And since when did crawling take so long? But everything else was calm. Aeden should be okay. I stood up at the other end and watched her bend down to start making her way across the building. Michel and I didn't say a word. He must have been thinking the same thing. She was part way across by now, moving steadily. And then, we heard it. A whooshing sound. A funny whooshing sound that seemed to be coming from above. Couldn't be the soldiers. They don't whoosh. They stamp, stomp, and shoot. But what the heck was it?

Then, something brushed across my face and I knew what it was. Bats! They were coming back in to roost, or whatever it was they did when they were done eating bugs in the night. Bats! Aeden was going to a have a freak-out fest that would make history.

"I've got to crawl back and get her," I said to Michel.

"It's too dangerous. I don't think the planks will support both of you."

"I have no choice. She's going to go crazy and let go."

If one tiny mouse could cause screams that shook the building, I hated to think what was about to happen next. Bending down, I edged my way forward, not paying attention to the fact that I'd have to crawl backwards once I reached her. Slowly, inch by inch, I made my way toward her. She seemed oblivious to the darting bats that were circling us. "Good," I thought. "Maybe she didn't notice. Maybe she's so intent on crawling, that she doesn't see them."

I reached out my hand and grabbed her wrist, but she shook it off and whispered.

"What are you doing? You could get us both killed."

"I came here to help YOU!"

"I was crawling just fine."

"Yeah, but I thought you might be afraid of the...you know..." And then I said it. "The bats. The bats that are coming back into the tower."

Aeden stared straight at me as if I had lost my mind.

"I'm not scared of bats. What made you think I'd be scared of bats? I actually like bats. They're so cute with those weird little faces and big ears."

I couldn't believe what I was hearing. *What made me think you'd be scared of bats, Aeden? Oh, I don't know...maybe the fact that a mouse the size of a pea made you go freaking ballistic on the tower stairwell?*

I swear, at that moment, I could have pushed her off the plank myself.

Chapter Forty-Two: Aeden

Ryn was really pissed, I could tell. But I was doing fine. I did thank him but he was too busy grumbling as he inched his body backwards. He didn't even offer me a hand as I stood up once I reached the end of the crawlspace. Monsieur Chastain took a bit longer. I think all of the strain was getting to him. But now, we were all safely across and ready to continue.

The crawlspace opened into a rectangular room with a stairwell. At least it wasn't spiral. But, it went straight down with narrow steps, the kind that makes it easy for you to lose your footing. And believe it or not, I actually welcomed the thought of going back into the sewers. No more steep drop-offs, no more climbing. Just sewage.

I hugged the wall as I followed Michel and Ryn down the steps, one foot at a time. Michel was already way ahead of us. Nothing seemed to unnerve him. I could hear Monsieur Chastain's steady breathing as we headed to the depths of the Bastille once again. It was an arduous descent and my body was still reeling from that long crawl. The sound of steady breaths was reassuring but then, something went terribly wrong. I heard a quick gasp and turned my head. Even in the dark, I could see a tall, slender figure charging towards Monsieur Chastain. Her voice clawed, like fingers on a chalkboard, and whatever it was she said, echoed down the stairs.

"Julien, it is your turn to suffer."

Then, she lunged at Monsieur Chastain, who had to steady himself against the wall.

"Fast, Renaud and Anjenet," he yelled. *"Get down these stairs as fast as you can."*

There was no time for me to stop and look. I had to keep moving. Ryn thundered in front of me taking two or three steps at a time. I could barely manage the one. Behind me, the woman continued to shriek. Then I heard Michel's voice from below.

"Watch out, Monsieur Chastain. She has a knife!"

Monsieur Chastain was trying to reason with her. At least that's what it sounded like.

"Stop this, Margaux. Stop this. You will get us all killed."

The struggle continued but there was no more talking. Just heavy breaths and some movement on the steps. Ryn jumped to the bottom of the stairs just as a knife landed next to him. Any sound that it could have made was absorbed by the hard dirt floor. But there was enough light from the large torches on the walls to see that the knife was dripping with blood. I was pressed against the wall perpendicular to the stairwell, eyes fixed on the lady who, by now, was grabbing at Monsieur Chastain's hair. He seemed to be holding her off with one hand. Had she stabbed him? Was it his blood on the knife?

Michel started for the stairs but it was too late. With a quick shove from his good hand, Monsieur Chastain unleashed the woman and held his breath as she fell backwards to the ground. None of us wasted any time to see if she was still breathing, because at that very moment, the Bastille shook with all the fury and intensity of a full blown war. Someone was firing the cannons and the sound was deafening.

Chapter Forty-Three: Ryn

Great. A madwoman. A madwoman on a staircase. It was like having front row seats to an old Alfred Hitchcock movie. All we needed was a shower curtain and some music. It was impossible to turn my eyes away. I heard her yell *"Julien"* and Monsieur Chastain called her *"Margaux."* So she was alive after all. Just not in her room. Or was she hiding there all along? Ugh. That's a thought that would creep me out. This was worse than a Hitchcock movie.

I could see the blood dripping from Monsieur Chastain's neck but before I could say anything, he spoke.

"It is all right, Renaud. Just a scrape. The knife didn't penetrate. Now stop worrying and let's go."

Michel and Aeden were already on the other side of the room under an archway that led to another corridor.

"Listen carefully," Michel exclaimed as we continued to walk. *"This is the only safe way out of here, but it is below the sewers."*

Below the sewers! What the heck could possibly be below the sewers? I wanted a full scale drawing of the Bastille and its plumbing system, but all I was going to get was a quick "do as I say" from Michel. The cannons were getting louder. They were firing off more of them. Must be the unexpected crowd had arrived. And damn them! They arrived sooner than I had figured. Sooner than Mademoiselle Claudine told us they would. Damn it! Didn't they know their own history?

I started to say something, but Michel continued to talk.

"Just down this hallway is a small door that appears as if it opens into one of the garderobes, but it is a chute. A chute that is used for refuse and excess water, but wide enough for a body. One must lay straight back with hands to the side. It will take us directly into The Seine. Hold your breath at all costs. You will be plunged under the surface of the river. Do not open your mouths until you swim to the top."

Great. I couldn't even sit through "The Abyss," without choking. Now I'm told we have to continue playing "Chutes & Ladders" under the Bastille? Sure, Aeden and I know how to swim, but sliding in the dark on a sewage chute is just too much to ask.

"Isn't there another way?" I said. *"I mean, couldn't we just make a run for it?"*

At this juncture in time I would have taken my chances with a million cannons and a legion of angry peasants. But, as Michel pointed out, *"The odds of survival are non!"*

"What about the odds of survival on that chute?"

"Do not worry. It moves fast and once you are underwater, you will surface quickly."

"And how do you know this?"

"Because you were right all along, my friend. This is not my first time in the Bastille."

Monsieur Chastain put his arms around Aeden and me, drawing us close to his face. I could see the dried blood on his neck and for a second, I had the strangest thought. Then, he spoke softly to us.

"Do not be scared. It will be over quickly. And once we have surfaced, we shall swim to the north shore. From there, we will seek refuge and move further north, out of the city."

There was no way I could explain any of this to my sister. Hell, I couldn't even process it myself! We were actually going to go shooting ourselves down some sewage trough only to wind up in the biggest garbage dump of them all—The Seine. If the ride down doesn't kill us, the germs will. I'll bet there are all sorts of flesh eating bacteria down there just waiting to be discovered. Cannons firing and armed revolutionaries seemed almost welcome. Then, I thought of something else. Did anyone bother to pick up the crazy woman's knife?

Chapter Forty-Four: Aeden

Monsieur Chastain kept hugging me, and Ryn kept trying to whisper something in my ear. I knew this wasn't good. Whatever we were about to do would make everything else we've done seem simple by comparison.

The hallway was damp and reeked of rotten garbage. Michel seemed to be looking in the semi-darkness for a specific door and I finally heard what Ryn was saying—"wet and wild."

"Wet and Wild." Was he referring to the fact that this whole business in the Bastille was some sort of adventure? "Wet and Wild." That's not the kind of language he uses when he describes stuff. And then it all made sense. He wasn't describing something. He was giving me a clue to something. "Wet & Wild" was the water park just outside of Portland. We use to take school trips there at the end of the year. Why in the world would he mention that?

And then I knew. Water! We were going to be doing something with water. I figured it was another moat, but when Michel pulled open the small door opposite the only oil lamp in the corridor, I realized that it was much worse. One by one, we would be taking that chute to the very depths of the Bastille. My knees began to wobble and I felt as if I would faint.

"We must go now," Michel commanded. *"There is little time."*

I watched as he leaned back, placing one foot at a time onto the chute, his hands holding the metal trough. Then, he put his arms at his side, and in an instant, he slid out of our sight and into the darkness. I could hear him yell *"Au Revoir Artois"* and then he was gone. I let out a breath that seemed to fill the air. *Artois.* Was that another name on the wall?

Ryn mouthed the words, "You'll be okay," as he grabbed the slide and climbed on. I mouthed back, "You jerk!" At least my anger stopped me from shaking. Monsieur Chastain helped me position myself on the chute. I was laying straight back with hands at my side when I heard a commotion. A horrible commotion. Like people tearing at each other. I couldn't turn around. I could only take a deep breath as I plunged into absolute darkness, waiting for it all to end.

I knew Monsieur Chastain would be directly behind me, but what if something happened to him? I had no way of knowing. I was moving so quickly that all I could think about was the awful sensation of a sliding free fall into what? Hard ground? Water? I tried to brace myself and took a deep breath. I don't even remember exhaling.

The icy plunge came so fast, so unexpected that it stung every part of my body. I was underwater. Stretching my arms out in front of my body, I started to swim to the surface. The pull on the back of my head came so fast, so furious that I thought I had gotten stuck in something. A vent? A filter? This wasn't a swimming pool. This was The Seine. I reached my hand behind my head only to have someone grab my wrist and start to pull me further under.

Was that the commotion I heard? The thought of opening my eyes into dark, murky water was repulsive. Still, someone was trying to drown me. Eyes open or not, I started to fight back. I kicked my legs as hard as I could, trying to deal with the water resistance and my assailant. Then, I managed to turn myself around so that I could face whoever it was and fight straight-on and not from behind.

But they were strong. And they fought dirty. Grabbing my hair so hard that my tears felt warm against the cold river water. Still, I tried to use one arm to move myself closer to the surface. If I could only get a breath, I might be able to survive. By now my body was entangled with theirs. And their grip was strong, pulling the front of my shirt so that making my way to the surface would be impossible.

I needed air and I needed it at that moment. But my combatant had other plans and I could only struggle relentlessly until the filthy river water began to fill my lungs.

Chapter Forty-Five: Ryn

I felt awful for Aeden as I entered the chute and held my breath. But what choice did I have? Did any of us have? At least this would be fast and over with in no time. We'd hit the water, surface and swim to shore. Not the most detailed of plans, but hey, at least it was something. I tried to pretend that this was just another water park ride, but the sewage that had made its way down the trough for centuries left a permanent stench in the air. I held my breath. Years of use had made the slide slippery and fast. I was underwater in seconds. But once I surfaced, I realized that everything we'd been through in the Bastille was just a preview to the nightmare that had started in the streets.

Damn it! Where was Aeden? Or Michel for that matter? Or Monseiur Chastain? At first, the river just looked as if it were filled with garbage. But garbage doesn't swim. Holy crap! The place was filled with people, all trying to get to the Bastille from the south side of the city. No wonder I couldn't find my sister or anyone, it was just a mass of bobbing heads and movement. I could hear people screaming from both sides of the river, only to have their voices drowned out by the cannon fire.

The Seine. Why didn't anyone ever mention the river? I just thought the citizens broke into the fortress from the front courtyard. Stupid history book. It just gave me the abridged version! Now I'm in a stinking river trying to find my sister and the one relative whose life will ultimately determine whether or not I get born. But the family line could continue with the real Renaud, couldn't it? But what if something already happened to him? No way out of this mess.

The banks of the river were chaotic. People charging, yelling, fighting. Some were holding lit torches. Terrific. They'll burn the place down before I find anyone. Everything around me was moving at such a frenetic pace that I hardly had time to think. And that's when Edouard Favreau found me.

Someone must have opened his cell, because here he was, in the water, going straight for my neck.

"Chastain swine. I couldn't resist the opportunity to make sure you drown."

My mind was spinning. *So, this guy manages to get out of his cell, get to the street on the north side of the Bastille, and what does he do? Sees me and decides to jump into the water to kill me. Talk about the need for revenge*...I had to act fast. As he grabbed my neck, I gave him a full-fledged kick to the groin that should have been documented in every textbook. He fell back into the water for just an instant, enough time for me to start swimming away. But the one thing I didn't count on, was the fact that he wasn't alone in this endeavor. Apparently, others relished the thought of a bloated, dead Chastain floating in the Seine. Well, it wasn't going to be me, or any of us for that matter.

But I hate unfair fights. Especially water fights. At least two others had come to the aid of Edouard, and they were strong. The first guy grabbed one of my legs and started to pull me under while the second yanked on my opposite arm. I found myself kicking, flailing and screaming. Screams that Michel heard a few yards away. He moved like a shark, single minded and fast. Within seconds, he had joined the struggle.

"You are so much trouble, Chastain. Still, I owe you."

And then, I finally understood the meaning of the word melee. Michel fought like a river rat. Biting, pulling, kicking and jabbing. The water splashed with such intensity that it was impossible to see anything. I was now out of anyone's grip but the fight wasn't over. Edouard and the other two men pushed down hard on our heads and punched at our chests. Water filled my mouth and I spit wildly at the air.

If these guys don't kill me, the bacteria will. Is there Black Plague bacteria in this river? Hell, I can't stop to think about it.

I could see someone else swimming our way. Two against four. We'd never survive. The only thing we could do was try to swim away, but we couldn't get around them fast enough. And then, the fourth person arrived and I knew it was over.

Chapter Forty-Six: Aeden

My arms were getting weak from fighting and my muscles ached from the resistance of the water. I tried to subdue my assailant but it was no use. Whoever it was, they seemed to have unwavering strength. My only hope was that Ryn, Michel or Monsieur Chastain would get to me before it was too late. I had been keeping my eyes closed, mainly out of fear. But with my head barely above the water and a choke hold on my neck, I needed to know just who wanted to kill me.

The water and muted sunlight stung my eyes but I got a good look. It was Margaux. The woman on the staircase. The one who tried to kill Monsieur Chastain. She wasn't dead after all. She was very much alive and consumed by rage.

"Sales porcs Chastain petits. Prenez votre dernier souffle."

I didn't need a translator. She called me a filthy little pig and made her intent perfectly clear. She wanted me to drown. What I did need, was someone to come to my rescue. With one quick pull, she grasped my shirt again, only this time, even stronger. I was going under and I wasn't about to get up. My hands remained flat on my sides, against the material of my skirt. And just then, one of them brushed against something sharp.

The needle! The embroidery needle that Lizette had placed in my bag. Oh my gosh, I had forgotten all about it. Carefully, so as not to lose my grip, I pulled it out and jabbed it at every part of her body that I could reach. I wasn't about to die in a murky river after all, I was going to fight her every step of the way.

I held that needle and continued my assault on her body as if nothing else mattered. Her mouth spewed out a litany of words. Words Ryn would have a hard time translating.

"Merde embulante!" "Laide de la vache!"

But I didn't stop. Not even when I saw trickles of blood down her arms and neck. Still, she fought me like a savage. Every bit of hate and agony that she felt for Monsieur Chastain was now being unleashed on me. I was *Anjenet* for all she knew, and that was enough.

With one hand wide open she came at my face, but was it her hand or the cold, silver tip of a blade? I couldn't be sure. Before I could react, the water entered my mouth and forced me to close my eyes. Then, panic! I felt someone's grip on my waist. Another prisoner with a vendetta? I tried to prick their hand with the needle when I heard a familiar voice.

"Tout va bien, Anjenet. Juste nager loin. Nager jusqu'à la rive."

It was Monsieur Chastain. He had found me. Told me to do something. Swim maybe? His arm was strong enough to back me away from Margaux while taking the brunt of her fury. I started to dog paddle my way across the river. Ryn and Michel had to be nearby. But where? My tired arms moved in monotonous strokes and as I leaned my head from side to side I could see that the river was teeming with people. No wonder they couldn't find me.

Both sides of the shore looked like parades gone awry. People running, screaming, fighting. And the torches. Why were they carrying lit torches in broad daylight? Off in the distance I could see the Bastille. I hadn't realized how far into the river that chute had taken us. At first it just looked like lots of movement, but then, I could see that people were climbing everywhere. Over the gates, onto the stone walls, and even onto the towers.

The shore was as dangerous as the river. I looked back to where Monsieur Chastain and Margaux had been but I couldn't see them. Had she drowned? Had he...I didn't want to think about it. People were treading water, swimming, and doing whatever they could to get across the Seine and into the Bastille.

This wasn't like a lake or the beach. The riverbank was steep. No easy way to crawl out. Yet, here I was, soaked and saturated with the scum of the water on my skin, trying to figure out just what to do. As I looked up, I realized that people were being helped ashore by the tumultuous crowd in the street. Hands were offered to hoist them up. More people to get swept into the crowd. And I was next.

A large, stocky man leaned over the bank and reached for my arm. In an instant, I had joined the revolt.

Chapter Forty-Seven: Ryn

My neck and jaw were taking the brunt of this punishment and my mouth kept filling up with water. I was swallowing every possible disease that had been harboring in the river since the middle ages. Next to me, Michel was punching furiously. But those men knew how to fight and they weren't giving up. Forger, indeed! That Edouard was probably some sort of murderer. And now someone else was joining them.

I could see his head moving side to side in the water as he swam toward us. Still, I used every muscle I could to defend myself against his friends or whoever these guys were. Edouard was now inches from my face and the only thing I could do was spit water at him.

Good, you filthy slime! Hope you choke on a parasite! But he was fast, grabbing me by the neck just as the other guy swam up from behind. I reached my leg back to kick at him, fighting the water resistance, but I never got the chance. In a split second, he had yanked Edouard from the hair and pulled him under.

Holy crap! It's Monsieur Chastain! I'm not about to drown in the cesspit after all! The fight was evened up. Michel and I actually had a chance. I took a deep breath and kept punching. Water splashed everywhere. There was no way of knowing who I was hitting and where. I just kept struggling.

I couldn't seem to get my hands above the water to land a decent punch. But this wasn't a prizefight. This was a dirty scuffle in a river and no rules applied. I reached out my hand and pulled on the waist that belonged to one of the men. Then I punched his stomach so hard that my hand hurt. He backed off. Enough for me to spin around and land a few quick jabs at the guy who was tangled up with Michel.

Were we winning? Suddenly, I felt something crash against the back of my head before it hit the water. Edouard. It was Edouard and Monsieur Chastain had managed to knock out some of the guy's teeth. I could see blood running down his mouth and neck.

"It's not over, Chastain. Your family will pay for this," Edouard uttered as he tried to tread water.

Meanwhile, Michel continued to defend himself against the two men who had joined Edouard. With a quick side stroke, I managed to position myself behind one of them and jab him under the ear. By now, Monsieur Chastain had taken on the other guy and it was just a matter of minutes before the guy started swallowing water and choking.

But what I never expected was the thing that always happens in horror movies. The monster, that everyone thought was dead, manages to return and scare the crap out you. In this case, that insane Margaux. She came out of nowhere swimming furiously towards us. And with her long, tangled hair soaking wet, she looked disheveled and wild. The fact that a knife was clamped firmly between her teeth was the *pièce de résistance.*

Damn it! Why didn't any of us go back and get that stupid knife when it was lying right next to her in the stairwell? Now it's going to wind up on someone's throat.

Teeth or no teeth, Edouard still had plenty of fight left in him. So, if it wasn't bad enough that Margaux wanted us dead, she now had a few allies. They lunged at us from all angles, splashing, grabbing and tearing. But we fought back, too.

Suddenly, Margaux took the knife from her mouth and stabbed it right into Monsieur Chastain's arm, just as he was about to pull me away. All I could see was a massive amount of blood spilling into the water. I turned to face him, just as the knife plunged directly into the middle of his neck. I twisted myself around to get a better look and that's when I realized that she had killed the wrong man in all of the confusion.

Edouard fell backwards into the water and sank slowly; his arms and legs were the last to go under. The two men who were with him tried to get a hold of the body. That gave me and Monsieur Chastain the few seconds we needed to get away. I started to look for Aeden but it was impossible. The people who were storming the streets of Paris had turned the river into a congested hell hole of bodies. Even if she were right next to me, I wouldn't have been able to see her.

Everyone was splashing, swimming, fighting or trying not to drown. I'd seen crowds like this before, in water parks, but the screeches I heard weren't from laughter. They were from terror; and I felt those first pings of shock, too, when I realized I might never find my sister.

Off in the distance, I could swear someone was screaming out my name. Or was it my imagination? "*Renaud! Renaud!*" Aeden? Was she yelling for me? I scanned both sides of the river bank, squinting and looking for her.

The voice got louder. Even with the noise and rumbling from the streets, I could hear the name. "*Renaud! Over here! Renaud!*"

I looked at the south side of the river, expecting to see Aeden. Hoping to see Aeden... And sure enough, a young girl was waving her arms frantically. But something was off. I was too far from shore to get a good look, but I know when things aren't right. And this wasn't. Still, I kept looking, even though my eyes were burning from the water.

On the bank of the river, screaming her lungs out, was Lizette. Anjenet's servant.

"I wouldn't let the carriage leave without Monsieur Chastain."

She had come back for us.

Chapter Forty-Eight: Aeden

I felt the sharp tug on my arm as the man started to lift me from the river. He reached down, grabbed me by the waist and gave quick pull. Then, before I could say anything, he was gone, replaced by a throng of angry citizens, pushing their way up the street. I lunged forward and kept moving, dazed. There was no way to turn around. The crowd had gotten enormous.

It was a cacophony of chants, screams and bellowing. People were waving muskets and swords. Some were holding torches. Others, flags. But all of them seemed to be shouting at once. The noise was like a slow crescendo and I tried not to think about what was coming next. A few times, I turned around, hoping to work my way back to the river edge but it was impossible.

As we got closer to the Bastille, smoke started to fill the air. Strong, acrid, smoke. The guards were still firing the cannons and each thunderous blow shook the ground. Still, the crowd moved forward like some sort of wild beast that had been chained up for far too long. Like it or not, I had become part of that beast.

The crowd was now gaining momentum, running wildly. For the first time in my life I knew what the words “out of control” meant. I had to find a way back. Ryn and the others would be looking for me. I was certain of it. But there was no way they would find me in this chaos. Someone shoved me from behind and yelled.

“Se dépêcher!”

Blindly, I stumbled forward. The smoke was getting thicker. I covered my mouth with my hand and kept moving. My feet were numb and my wet clothes stuck to me. Every inch of my body felt raw and exposed. But here, in the middle of this madness, no one noticed. No one cared. I just kept moving. For how long, I don’t know. Up ahead I could see the Bastille. We had reached the first courtyard. Guns were firing everywhere and the one large crowd had now broken into groups that fought among themselves. The soldiers who were still guarding the Bastille joined the mayhem. I was brushed aside, tossed, kicked, and thrown against the courtyard wall as I tried to avoid the mob scene that was unfolding at a terrifying pace.

The irony wasn't lost on me. We had spent hours trying to escape from that fortress and when we finally succeeded, I found myself hurled back to the very spot where I had entered a day ago.

The mob was relentless. I had to find a way out before I got crushed to the ground. One slip, one fall, and I'd be trampled. And Ryn. I had to find Ryn. This was worse than the last time history separated us. At least in Arizona, a revolution was not taking place. The last time, I jumped from a train. But where could I jump now?

And then, out of the corner of my eye, I realized I had a way out. There were ropes dangling from the towers. Ropes that may have been used to lower prisoners to their escape. I only needed to climb for a bit and hang on to a garderobe or turret until I could see a break in the crowd and maybe make a run for the river. I knew things were going to get worse. The river was my only option. But right now, it was too far away. I edged my way through the outer wall, pressing my body against it as the people around me continued to fight.

A quick sprint and I was at the tower, my hands hungrily reaching for the rope. Oblivious to the sharp pricks from the twine, I grasped the knotted cord and pulled myself up, wrapping my feet around the bottom as the fibers tore into my flesh. Slowly, I crawled up the side of the Bastille, wondering which tower it was. The one with the moat? The crisscross ledge? Or perhaps it was the one we hadn't entered. No matter, I was outside now, watching a war that seemed to be escalating with every second.

A small window ledge was just a few feet above me. No time to think. I refused to stop climbing until I found myself pressed against the metal bars that obscured the glass. My feet rested on the narrow bricks and I caught my breath, only to cough uncontrollably. Below me, guns were being fired and the air filled with smoke. The odor of gunpowder permeated everything.

How long could I remain here? Would someone shoot me randomly? My mind was racing with thoughts and nothing made sense. I refused to let go of the rope. It was the only thing that separated me from an untimely death in a century I wanted to forget. Below me, nothing but smoke and madness. I tried to adjust my footing on the brick ledge, holding on to the rope with one hand, and the metal bars with the other. Then, the unthinkable. One of the bricks loosened under my feet and fell to the ground, smashing bits of clay and mortar into the crowd. I could hear people scream.

"Détruire la Bastille – brique par brique!"

It was close enough to Spanish, that I understood what they were saying.

"Down with the Bastille – brick by brick!"

And then, everyone seemed to rush to the towers at once, grabbing on ledges, using the jutting bricks from the garderobes to climb, whatever it took to reach the window sills, where they began to loosen the bricks and hurl them to the ground.

My God, what have I done?

Chapter Forty-Nine: Ryn

I kept forcing my arms over my head as I swam towards Lizette. She remained fixed, like a statue, watching every stroke I made. Behind me, Monsieur Chastain was swimming furiously. He had heard her, too. Lizette had managed to come back with the carriage. He would be safe. They'd make it to Normandy. I just needed to convince him to go with her. Then, I could concentrate on finding Aeden. With any luck, maybe Michel had already succeeded.

"Hurry Renaud! Hurry!" Lizette sounded frantic.

Before I could respond, Monsieur Chastain answered for me.

"WAIT! Seek refuge and wait. We will return to the shore. But we must find Anjenet first! I will not leave without my daughter."

"Oui Monsieur," Lizette yelled back. *"The horses and carriage are safe for now, but hurry!"*

Then, she turned away and ran. Talk about lousy timing. This really wasn't the appropriate moment to tell poor Monsieur Chastain that we really weren't his kids after all, and that if he wanted his family line to continue, he needed to get into that damn carriage. Like he'd ever believe me. The guy was really protective of Aeden. Anyone could see that. There was no way he was going anywhere without her. And frankly, I was getting a bit freaked out myself.

"Renaud!" he exclaimed as he swam towards me, *"Thank God you are all right. But poor Anjenet, poor Anjenet... I saw her out of the corner of my eye getting swept into the crowd. She was on the north shore. Someone pulled her up the bank and she has no way to turn back. The crowd is too large, too dangerous. Their very movements are forcing her back to the Bastille!"*

"What about Michel?" I asked.

"He saw her first. He's trying to reach her and we must do so as well. Hurry! Swim to the other shore!"

"And the woman who tried to kill you?"

"She is no longer a threat, now hurry!"

My body moved automatically, maneuvering itself around the other swimmers who really wanted to take part in this nightmare. I just wanted to find my sister and get us the hell out of here before the real flashpoint began. But I had no idea of the timing, and besides, none of it seemed to match the history books anyway. I just knew that at some point a bunch of angry citizens were going to seize the governor of the Bastille and drag him through the streets of Paris. Oh, and did I mention that they were also going to start chopping off heads and annihilating anyone in sight? Yeah, that, too.

"Renaud, quick! Michel is already over the bank and into the crowd. We must follow!"

Cannons were firing. And people were screaming—waving swords and muskets. They charged towards the Bastille faster than any running back I'd ever seen. We scrambled up the bank and took our places in the crowd. Yep, we were welcomed into the insanity without as much as a "Hello." It was so fast and so crazy, that I didn't even have time to think about how miserable I felt in wet, dripping clothes.

Up ahead I could see the back of Michel's head. His straight dark hair was still soaking wet and hung down past his shoulders. Monsieur Chastain and I tried to take larger strides to catch up. *But was Michel going there to find Aeden or to be part of the revolt? I mean, the guy kept his promise. He got us out of the Bastille. He didn't owe us anything else. So why was he going back?*

I couldn't let my mind dwell on it. Besides, why worry about something you can't control. What I could control was my focus and I started scanning the crowd for Aeden. She had to be heading straight towards the front courtyard. Around me, the crowd starting chanting.

"Couper la gorge! Couper la gorge!"

Someone poked me. They expected us to chant, too. Terrific. Nothing like marching down a street yelling "Cut their throats! Cut their throats!" I swallowed whatever saliva was left in my mouth, and with the first syllable I uttered, I had taken sides in this revolution.

My sneakers were starting to dry and felt like pressed cardboard against my feet. True, it was a rather petty thing to be concerned about at a time like this, but hell—my feet were killing me! We were still blocks away from the Bastille and Aeden was nowhere in sight. Monsieur Chastain and I just kept pace with the crowd. Not like we had a choice. It was the ugliest organized rioting in the streets I could ever imagine. And worst of all, we were part of it.

Suddenly, I saw Michel pointing to something. He kept moving his arm above his head and pointing with one finger. I felt like doing something with a finger, too, but no one would understand. By now, we were getting closer to the building itself and Michel kept waving and pointing. Around us, the chant continued.

"Couper la gorge! Couper la gorge!"

We were entering the courtyard. Smoke everywhere! People were shooting off guns and waving swords. Monsieur Chastain and I still had the daggers we got from the cell with the dead guys, but I hardly felt like waving mine in the air.

Michel continued to point. He had seen something on the corner tower. I squinted to get a better look. Some nut job had climbed up a rope and the crowd was cheering from below. I looked at the other towers and more people were doing the same thing. But as we got closer, I heard a different chant.

"Détruire la Bastille – brique par brique!"

So that's what they were doing. Throwing bricks! Tearing off loose bricks and throwing them! Apparently the nutcase from the first tower had started it. Well, everything has to start somewhere...

Just then, I heard Monsieur Chastain let out a horrific scream. He was staring right up at the tower. I edged myself forward, this time muttering the new chant. Then, I saw for myself what had scared the living crap out of him.

The nutcase on the first tower was my sister and there was thick smoke all around her.

Chapter Fifty: Aeden

The smoke was so thick below me that all I could see were the top of people's heads. Guns were being fired off everywhere, only now I wasn't alone on the tower. Others had scrambled up the brick wall, too, using every available crevice and ledge. Above me, more bricks were being hurled.

I was trapped. No way up, no way out. With bricks raining down, I'd be killed trying to climb to the roof of the tower. And if I were to jump below, I'd never survive. My fingers were beginning to shake as I held on to the metal bars that were gradually coming loose from the window's edges. It was only a matter of time. I had to act fast, but my mind froze.

Suddenly, I felt the sting of a hard object hitting my arm. Too small for a brick, but someone threw something at me. Was I now the new target in this uprising? The smoke was starting to dissipate and I forced myself to look down. In the madness of the crowd, I recognized Michel. He had used a small rock to get my attention. By now, my fingers were shaking badly and my legs were wobbling. Bricks were being hurled everywhere, and in the midst of all the chaos, Michel screamed at me as loud as he could.

"Aller en bas Anjenet. La corniche est en ruine. Je vais vous attraper. Saute MAINTENANT!"

Whatever he was saying got lost in the cacophony of the crowd and my inability to understand. Still, he screamed.

"SAUTE MAINTENANT!"

And then, in an instant, I knew what he meant. And I knew why he was so adamant. The ledge was crumbling beneath me.

JUMP DOWN NOW !

My extremities were shaking so badly that it felt as if I was about to lose control of my body. And then, the entire metal railing came loose in my hand, the weight of it forcing me to let go of the rope. I fell headfirst, inches behind the metal that had already reached the ground.

I had always thought a fast fall would be just that—fast. But it wasn't. Everything seemed to be happening in slow motion. My body was stretched out in the air and I could see the ground getting closer. But it wasn't the hard dirt that scared me. It was the tips of the swords that were still being waved in the air. *It will be a quick death. The blade will slice my throat and I'll be part of history*. I closed my eyes and willed myself to faint. *If I faint, I won't know I'm dead. Faint, Aeden, Faint.*

My body felt as if it were accelerating, making up for the slow motion as gravity got stronger. I held my breath. A few more seconds and it would be over...And then, I felt a crushing sensation on both sides of my waist, moving tighter and tighter into my stomach. A piercing grip that meant only one thing—*this is what the last breath feels like*. And my ears, they starting ringing until all of the sounds around me had disappeared. *Finally, I fainted.*

Someone was slapping my cheeks and forcing me to stand. I coughed as I inhaled the smoke around me. It was Michel's arms that had caught me. I looked into his face and could see the combination of terror and resolve. Around us, the madness continued and the noise had returned to my ears.

"Venez, Anjenet, nous devons atteindre la paroi latérale et de faire notre chemin de retour à la rivière!"

He was motioning to the side wall and the river. This time I got it. We had to reach that wall and jump in. Our only hope.

My feet felt like rubber and my senses were all out of whack. I latched on to his hand and refused to let go. We started to skirt the crowd by bending, weaving and forcing ourselves to the few open spaces we could find. Around us, people were chanting and screaming. More gunfire. Only I no longer heard the sounds of the cannons.

My thoughts raced to Ryn and Monsieur Chastain. Were they still in the river? Is that where we were headed? I could feel the bones in Michel's hand, that's how tight I was holding it. He used his free arm to nudge and wedge his way around the crowd. By now, the chanting was unbearable. And worse yet, I recognized the words.

"Couper la gorge! Couper la gorge!"

La Gorge. Throat. Throats? I think this is what Ryn said I was screaming on the plane. Something about cutting people's throats. Suddenly, I felt nauseous. Sickeningly nauseous. I bent over, as if I were about to explode and that's the moment I heard another chant. Its words so terrifying that my entire body went cold. Not from the wet clothing, not from the fall, but from what I knew was about to happen the minute I recognized the string of words.

"Couper la gorge Julien Chastain a!"

"Cut off Julien Chastain's throat!"

The crowd had seized upon its newest victim. And my stomach let loose on the bloody pavement.

Chapter Fifty-One: Ryn

By the time we edged closer to the tower, bricks were being hurled everywhere and the people with guns were firing them off at anything that moved. The rest of the crowd had turned into a stampede and it was headed straight for the inner courtyard. That was the one we saw from the window in the crazy lady's room. The courtyard with the gunpowder. It wouldn't take a rocket scientist to figure out what would happen if someone opened one of those barrels and put a torch to it. In my case, I already knew. I read that chapter in the history book and I knew we had to get the hell out of there fast!

But thanks to Aeden's bizarre Tarzan rope-swinging-what-the-heck-is-she-doing behavior, we had to get her off the tower first. I couldn't see anything in front of me between the smoke and the crowd. But Monsieur Chastain could. He was at least a foot taller and hadn't taken his eyes off that part of the Bastille from the minute he saw my sister.

"It is all right, Renaud. Look! Michel was able to catch her. We just need to--"

And in that second, everything changed. Someone recognized Monsieur Chastain. Someone with a vendetta. And, unfortunately, a loud voice.

"Julien Chastain. Aristocratic filth among us! Seize him and cut his throat!"

Then, the stragglers from the stampede turned and charged at us with their swords and guns. This time I didn't join the chant.

"Couper la gorge! Couper la gorge! Couper la gorge Julien Chastain a!"

Those maniacs didn't need an excuse to chop off Monsieur Chastain's head. They just needed proximity and I damn well was going to make sure they didn't get it. Our only way out was to join the way in and become part of the big stampede. We rushed that crowd head on—elbowing, bending, pushing, shoving, kicking and stomping. Techniques I've mastered from years of lunchroom lines. Only there was no meal at the other end.

It was only a few yards to the large courtyard but my body was getting bruised with every inch I took. These guys knew how to push, jab and elbow, too. Plus, they were wild with anger and frustration. And they were about to unleash it on Monsieur Chastain's neck when louder voices up ahead distracted them. Furious demands from a newly formed mob. Something about a bridge. Something important. And then I remembered the layout of the Bastille when we first arrived. We had crossed a bridge into the main courtyard. And now the bridge was up. No way to get in. That's what they were screaming about. At least it had nothing to do with Monsieur Chastain. We had slipped through that snarl with the hair still on our heads. But now what?

At least my sister was off the tower and with Michel. He'd be clever enough to figure out something, that is, if he were really on our side. But I was stuck. I couldn't leave Monsieur Chastain because our lives depended upon his, but I couldn't leave Aeden in such a desperate situation either. But sometimes, decisions aren't ours to be made and we just have to act in the moment.

And our moment was approaching a drawbridge with an angry mob. Their screams had turned into thunder and its roar was deafening. The weird thing was, I think I was yelling, too.

"Lower the bridge! Lower the bridge!"

I felt as if every bit of my insides were being squeezed as we pushed into each other and the crowd moved forward, drawbridge or not. Monsieur Chastain and I were side by side, our movements mimicking one another in this heated madness. Any minute now I expected all of us to plunge into the outer courtyard's moat. Whoever was on the other side had no intention of lowering the drawbridge. They'd have to be equally insane.

So the pushing, shoving, ranting and raving continued. Smoke mixed with the gray sky until there was no way of knowing which was which. The screams continued.

"Lower the bridge! Lower the bridge!"

At once, I started to fall forward and I had to catch myself. We were moving! Moving fast. Someone had lowered the drawbridge and we were swept into the frenzy.

I tried not to be pissed at Aeden. I mean, after all, it really wasn't her fault that she swam to the north side of the shore and got us back to where we started. She was disoriented, too. We all were. But geez, couldn't she at least have looked up, seen the Bastille and said to herself, "I need to be on the other side of river." Apparently not. And thanks to her, we were all going to get crushed or blown apart in this revolt.

I kept holding my breath waiting for someone else to recognize Monsieur Chastain. And then what? There was no place to run. I just hoped Michel would have brains enough to get him and Aeden back to the river. Around us people were screaming for blood and my only logical thought was that it would be more difficult to chop off someone's head while they were treading water in the Seine. At least my sister would have some sort of chance to live through this until I could reach her. Unfortunately, my mind kept re-playing a single sentence.

And then what?

And then what?

I admit it. I had no plan. How can you possibly have a plan when you're part of a frantic mob? We just kept moving forward until we had reached the inner courtyard. The citizens were still screaming for heads to be chopped off. But someone started a new chant and in that instant, I realized what Aeden had been trying to tell me all along about the names in the towers. They were the same ones that this crazy crowd was chanting.

ANJOU!

ARTOIS!

BEAULIEU!
CHASTAIN!
DAMPIERRE!
DREUX!
RICHELIEU!
VERMANDOIS!

Eight names. Eight aristocrats. And eight towers. There had to be some significance, but now wasn't the time for a history lesson. Especially with my family name in the middle of it.

It was madness. A frenetic crowd that would kill each other with just the right spark. And then, something flashed in my mind with all the clarity and composure of a well thought out dissertation. I had to create that spark in order to get us the hell out of here.

As the throng moved ahead and the momentum accelerated, I reached to the side and grabbed a lit torch from someone who had just lost his balance. Too bad! Mine now! Then, I shoved my way to the perimeter of the courtyard with Monsieur Chastain inches away. He must have thought I'd gone mad.

"Renaud, what are you doing?"

"It's our only way out. We've got to ignite some of these kegs. Go for the smaller ones. Use your dagger and pull off the lid. Spill some

gunpowder! Then, we make a run for the river!"

Maybe it was the determination on my face or that fact that I really did have a good idea, because seconds later, Monsieur Chastain pried the lid off of the first wooden box. I grabbed my dagger as well and got to the next barrel. It would have to be enough. We didn't have any time to waste. I wasn't sure if these kegs had fuses or not so the smaller barrels were our best bet. If they didn't have fuses, we could at least lift them, spill some gunpowder in a line, torch it and run. I'd seen it done a million times before on old TV westerns. I just hoped it wasn't some stupid Hollywood stunt because I didn't feel like getting my butt blown up in the process. All we had to do was ignite a keg or two. The blast and sparks would reach the others. I was betting on it!

Chapter Fifty-Two: Aeden

"Don't stop, Anjenet! Keep running!" Michel kept yelling at me as he pulled my arm. My feet felt heavy and numb as if everything around me had turned into one big stumbling block. He must have heard them yell out for Julien Chastain. Then why wouldn't he turn around?

"Faster, Anjenet. Faster!"

He had found a small break in the crowd and took advantage of it. Behind us, the stampede toward the inner courtyard continued. I knew my brother and Monsieur Chastain were there and I had to reach them.

With every bit of strength I could muster, I broke free of Michel's grip and made a run for the crowd.

"No Anjenet! NO!"

My eyes started to tear from the smoke but I knew I had to put some distance between me and Michel or he would prevent me from reaching Ryn and Monsieur Chastain. I ran until I finally reached the tail end of the first stampede. Another throng threatened to catch up. I just had to find them. I just had to....

And then, a blast with all the fury of hell shook the entire crowd and filled the air with thick, black smoke. People were falling, screaming and charging into one another. And that blast was just the beginning. It was followed by an explosion of such magnitude that my ears rang and my body shook.

By now, the crowd had lost its focus. At least for the moment. People were running and scurrying everywhere, but the thick smoke made it impossible to see anything. And then, just as it started to dissipate, another blast and another. These were smaller in intensity but still managed to produce so much soot and dirt in the air that everyone started coughing and choking at once.

In front of me, the Bastille had turned into an inferno. There were flames everywhere and anything people could grab was being hurled to the ground. If this crowd had one motive at all, it would be to demolish the place brick by brick. I paused to wipe my eyes and that familiar grip on my arm returned with full intensity.

"We must get out of here, Anjenet! We will burn in this hell."

I turned to see Michel's face. It was covered with soot and dirt from the blast. And I must have looked just as bad. He started to move me away from the confusion but I refused to budge. Somehow I had to make him understand what I needed to do, so I screamed out the only words that would matter.

"RENAUD! MONSIEUR CHASTAIN!"

Then, he did something I never expected. He shook me by the shoulders, pointed to the scorching building behind us, and threw his arm around me, pulling me further and further away from the mayhem.

"We cannot go back, Anjenet. It is too late."

I felt as if all I wanted to do was take my anger out at him. Pound on his chest. Kick at his feet and scream myself senseless. But all I did was start to sob as he grabbed my hand again and ushered me toward the river. I knew what he was thinking because I thought it, too. Renaud and Monsieur Chastain were dead. Killed in the blast. And if we didn't move quick enough, we would be next.

Chapter Fifty-Three:
Ryn

No one was near us when we located the fuse and lit the small keg. The last time I lit something was a fire back in 1930. *"Use a match, kid. This isn't the stone age." Yeah, Bill, but this is almost as bad and there are no matches. It's scarier with a torch.* My hand shook as I moved the flame closer to its target. Monsieur Chastain bellowed out a warning as we raced to the outer courtyard.

"Stay back! The gunpowder's been lit!"

Someone must have heard us because pandemonium broke loose with the crowd running in every direction. It was a small blast, not enough to do any real damage, but enough to create a mega diversion. No one was going to try to cut off Monsieur Chastain's head when an entire arsenal was about to explode behind them.

I don't even remember running. It all happened so fast. First, the small explosion, not much bigger than a decent fireworks display, but then...Holy Crap! That small keg must have ignited the others because the next blast was like a bomb. Everything shook at once and a bellow of black smoke filled the air. Monsieur Chastain got hold of my wrist and wouldn't let go.

For the first time in my life I understood what the expression, "on-auto-pilot" really meant. Some part of my brain must have been working because it forced my body to move. The other part, that stops to absorb and think about everything, was frozen. My feet thundered on the flat stones beneath me as we cleared the inner courtyard.

With the drawbridge down, we moved quickly across the wooden planks toward the outer tower where Aeden had jumped. Michel had caught her. That's what Monsieur Chastain said. Michel had caught her and she was all right. At least at that moment. But things were changing furiously here and there was no way of knowing what part of the crowd had devoured them.

We just kept running. It was too dangerous to stop, even for a second. My eyes filled with every piece of grit and dirt from the city. I couldn't even wipe them, that's how fast we were moving. Around us, the craziness and chaos had reached an all-time high. I know, because nothing made sense anymore. People were either fighting in small groups with all sorts of make-shift weapons and swords, or firing off the few muskets that still had ammunition.

Then, just as we had managed to clear the outer courtyard, Monsieur Chastain saw Aeden and Michel making a run for the river.

"Renaud! Quick! On your left! Anjenet and Michel. We must catch up! They'll be at the river!"

I started to respond when a new blast sent me falling face first into the ground. *Damn it! Had I started all of this? Well, what the heck, not like I had better options...*Chunks of dirt and rock stuck to my teeth as he yanked me up with one quick move and pulled me forward as he spoke.

"We can't lose them, Renaud. Hurry! They'll be at the river."

My mind was all over the place. *God knows what germs are in my mouth. Aeden's okay. She'll get to the river first. The river. "The Seine River is between 30 and 200 meters." I must've had to memorize that for French class. Meters. Crap! How many yards was that?*

How many meters in a yard? We must have crossed at the shortest distance when the chute spit us out. Can Aeden swim 200 meters? Can any of us? Monsieur Chastain drove through that crowd as if they were wooden pins and he was the toughest bowling ball in the lanes. And he wasn't thinking about the width of the Seine.

Furiously, as if hell were about to open up beneath us, we ran faster and faster. My chest started to hurt so badly that I hardly noticed the cramps in my legs. *So this is what a heart attack feels like.* And in the next instant—Aeden! She was right in front of us. I could have reached out and grabbed her if the screaming voice of a madwoman hadn't stopped me dead in my tracks.

"Die, Julien Chastain. Die!"

A string of curses so long it would fill a football field was hurled right at us from that insane Margaux who was obviously somewhere behind us, gaining momentum. But curses can't harm you. And if that was all the weaponry she had, then we were okay. I was only an arm's length from my sister when I realized that the crazy woman must have taken the "Sticks and Stones" rhyme seriously because she was now throwing all sorts of small projectiles our way.

"Don't stop, Renaud!" Monsieur Chastain yelled.

Like I was going to stop. First of all, I had nothing to throw. I mean, it wasn't as if I had time to stop and pick up chunks of debris. And even if I did, it would be like getting into a spitting contest with a pig. It would only make the pig angry. I kept running.

Aeden and Michel were gaining ground but we weren't far behind. I could see the river to our left and the banks were clear. I figured they'd jump in first and we'd be on their tails. But that was before Monsieur Chastain's jilted lover was able to land one well aimed shot. The rock clipped his head and he staggered forward for just a few feet, before regaining his composure.

"I am all right, Renaud. Just keep moving."

By now, the crowd had completely engulfed us, making it impossible to locate Aeden and Michel. Still, I knew they were headed straight for the river and all we needed to do was find the edge of the riverbank and jump. There weren't as many people wading across. Most of them were already taking part in the rioting and that was going on around us, not in the water. With fewer bodies swimming and bobbing about, I figured it would be relatively easy to find my sister.

It was my own fault for not paying closer attention to Monsieur Chastain as we bumped and shoved the people around us in a desperate attempt to escape. That rock must have hit him harder than I thought because he started to lose consciousness. And he started to lose it the minute he made the jump into the river.

Chapter Fifty-Four: Aeden

A splash and then a scream. A horrifying high-pitched scream that came from the other shore. Even the distance couldn't muffle it. Michel and I had just surfaced in the sharp, cold water when I heard it. Turning my head, I could see Lizette. It was as if she was waiting for something or someone. I thought by now she and the other servants would be on their way to Normandy. Isn't that what Ryn told her to do? But here she was, yelling frantically at the top of her lungs.

"L'aide de quelqu'un! Monsieur Chastain qui se noie!"

All I could make out was something about Monsieur Chastain, but Michel understood every word and with one stroke in the water, turned around to see what had made Lizette so hysterical. Before I could comprehend what I was seeing, he had already started swimming to the place where we had jumped in only minutes before.

Lizette was still screaming from the south shore. This time her words were directed at me but all I heard was my name.

"Anjenet....Anjenet!"

She kept motioning for me to swim towards her as I continued to tread water in the freezing river. The weight of my clothing was working against me. Michel was a few yards back by the north shore, swimming frantically. As I squinted into the hazy sunlight, I caught a glimpse of my brother just as he dove under the water. *Ryn. Diving. In the water. He's alive.* It took my mind a few seconds to piece together what had happened. I was still dazed and foggy from the tower jump and all the smoke that I had inhaled, but I knew one thing—someone was drowning and it had to be Monsieur Chastain. He wasn't killed in the blast. Something worse was happening. A slower, more painful death.

Michel's arms barely skimmed the surface of the water, that's how fast he moved. Ryn still hadn't surfaced and I could feel my entire body creating its own turbulence in the river. Lizette was still screaming, but this time she had company. Someone was standing next to her.

With each second, the anxiety I felt began to multiply. I was of no use to anyone in the water. The only thing I could do was head to shore before I lost the remaining bit of strength I had. Still, I couldn't take my eyes off the spot where I last saw Ryn. With large surface strokes I managed to move myself backwards, my eyes peeled on the water. *I'm sorry I said all those horrible things to you, Ryn. Just surface. Just surface.*

Then, as if on cue, Michel took a quick dive under. Seconds later, he emerged, but no Ryn and no Monsieur Chastain. I was numb, devoid of emotion and probably in shock. Had I lost my brother for good?

Michel dove under again and I kept watching the surface of the water. I was certain I had seen the exact spot where Ryn took that dive, but the water and the light play tricks on the mind. Perhaps that's what happened to Michel, because seconds later, Ryn emerged in an entirely different spot and he wasn't alone. He was fighting desperately to keep Monsieur Chastain's head above the water.

Michel spotted him immediately and swam over. By now, my brother had reached his exhaustion point. I know because I watched him back off as Michel took over, throwing his arm in front of Monsieur Chastain's head and moving slowly across the water, carrying the body as if it were a fragile piece of art.

And then, the colors started appearing. First dull mauves and pinks, then bright blasts of blue and indigo. Was this how time ends for us? Monsieur Chastain dead and Ryn and I never born? I inhaled the air, waiting for the inevitable void to consume me, but nothing happened. The colors dissipated and I could feel slight tremors in my extremities. I was freezing. Not dead. Not erased from life, just water logged and exhausted.

Ryn was inches from Michel and Monsieur Chastain, gliding across the river as if it was an Olympic trial and he had to be a top contender. Behind me, Lizette still stood at the shore, only she had stopped screaming. She had taken her cape off and was holding it straight out, presumably to use as a blanket once they got Monsieur Chastain to dry ground. The person standing next to her looked familiar. And then I remembered. It was Simeon. Renaud's servant. He had stripped off his topcoat and was also holding it. Both of them thought Monsieur Chastain was still alive.

Michel was still easing the body through the water. Ryn was only a few feet away. I was about to reach for the stone embankment as Lizette and Simeon rushed towards me. But something stopped them momentarily – the commotion from the Bastille side of the river. I turned my head around and saw a white flag being raised above the crowd. The government had surrendered. Screams and shots fired in the air replaced the cannons and explosions that had rocked the area just minutes before. Pandemonium had turned to victory.

I don't know if I was transfixed by what I was seeing or just so wiped out from trudging through the river, but I couldn't move from my spot in the water. My eyes were glued to the events taking place across the shore and for just a split second, I forgot about poor Monsieur Chastain, Michel and my brother.

The crowd seemed to separate on both sides of the flag. In the middle, someone was being dragged through the outer courtyard towards the Paris streets. I reached for the stone wall but felt so lightheaded that I started to slip back into the water. The colors were returning. Blues, indigos, pinks and yellows. And then, from a place where bizarre events and miscategorized information gets stored in the brain, I recalled one thing—a chapter title in my world history book. A chapter that I had long forgotten—"The Bloodbath Begins."

Chapter Fifty-Five:
Ryn

We were almost at the shore and I had no idea if Monsieur Chastain was dead or alive. *But he had to be alive, or I wouldn't be here, right?* But there was no time to think about all that theoretical stuff. Someone had reached over the embankment and was pulling Aeden out of the river. I felt crappy and relieved at the same time. Crappy, because I was so driven to make sure Monsieur Chastain was okay that I had forgotten about my sister. And relieved, because she was all right. I had lost sight of her in the mob scene, before she even made it to the river.

Behind me, on the Bastille shore, I could hear screams and shouts, but not like before. Something had changed. No time to take a look. The riverbank was almost within reach, and Michel would need help getting Monsieur Chastain to dry ground.

I could hear Simeon's voice as we got closer.

"Let me get you out of the water first, Renaud, and then we can lift Monsieur Chastain."

I turned to Michel and spoke. *"Can you still keep him afloat?"*

"Oui, Renaud. Let the man pull you out of the river."

It was so fast that I don't even recall scrambling up the rocks, but the next thing I knew, I was leaning over the bank, along with Simeon pulling Monsieur Chastain up from the Seine. Aeden and Lizette rushed over and the fear on their faces didn't make the situation any better. Thank God my sister didn't start screaming. That was all I needed.

Dislodged bits of conversations were getting stuck in my head. Nothing was there to filter them out. *If you want to be a lifeguard at the pool, Ryn, then you'd better take that CPR course. Stop procrastinating. ABC- Airway, Breathing, Circulation...or was that Compression? Rescue breaths, rescue breaths. Hope I don't ever have to do this unless some hot girl falls into the pool. Call 911. Call 911. There is no 911.*

Monsieur Chastain's body was cold. But we all were. I doubt it was instinct, but it sure as hell was automatic. Something kicked in somewhere in my brain and I began CPR. I could hear the muffled voices around me. Michel and the others must have thought I'd gone insane, throwing myself on my father's dead body and doing God-knows-what. But within seconds, a cough and then vomit. *Vomit. Why is there always vomit? But puke means he's alive. Alive!* I stepped back and caught my breath as Monsieur Chastain tried to raise his head. His voice was slow and raspy, but he didn't drown.

"Renaud, Anjenet, you are alive. We have made it."

Then, he passed out. Just like that. But he was breathing. And his breaths were steady. The guy wasn't going to die. "He'll have one heck of a headache when he wakes up," I thought to myself, "but he's not going to die."

Out of the corner of my eye I could see the commotion on the other side of the Bastille. The white flag waving and the crowd cheering. *Hurray for the winning team. We celebrate in style with decapitations. Sword or guillotine? All options considered.* But then I saw something that completely took me off guard. Something I hadn't expected so soon. It came in short blinks. The shoreline was changing and I could see some guy on a cell phone. Time was going to ripple back.

I know it sounds callus, but having Monsieur Chastain moving in and out of consciousness was the best thing that could have happened to us. I turned to Simeon and Lizette, speaking as fast as I could.

"Can you get our father to the carriage and out of the city?"

"Of course, Renaud," Lizette replied. "But we'll need some help carrying him."

I looked at Michel. He didn't owe us a thing. In fact, we owed him. He got us out of the Bastille, saved my sister and Monsieur Chastain. Even the "Three Musketeers" couldn't do all of that in a day. But was it just a scam so that he could cut our throats later? *No way. He had plenty of opportunity.* Reaching into my pocket, I took out the dagger we had removed from one of the dead guys in the cell. Then, I placed it in Michel's hand.

"I don't know why, but you kept your promise. And I must ask you to make another. Please go with the Chastain servants and see to it that Monsieur Chastain escapes the city. Take this dagger. You'll need it more than me."

Michel hesitated and then spoke.

"You and your sister are not going? I do not understand."

I took a deep breath and hoped the words came out right.

"We are not who you think we are. I tried to tell you the day we arrived at the Bastille. The real Renaud and Anjenet are in Normandy and their father's fate rests in your hands."

"I knew it!" Lizette exclaimed as she looked at Aeden. *"I knew you weren't Anjenet from the moment I helped you bathe. The real Anjenet has a birthmark on her lower shoulder and you do not."*

"Then why did you help us?" I said as Aeden struggled to figure out what was going on.

"Because there was something familiar about you, something I couldn't explain, but I knew you had come to help our master."

If I didn't think it would upset the whole time-continuum thing, I would have told her the truth. But then again, did I really need to risk being thrown into an 18th century insane asylum? I just kept my mouth shut.

Across the river, the Bastille was in flames and the cheering was out of control. I turned away and focused my attention on Michel.

"So will you help us?"

It was hard to read his face but I stood there, waiting for his answer.

"I gave you my word that I would get you out of the Bastille. I see no reason to break it now."

"But what about the families? The aristocrats? The Fleur-de-lis?"

"Take a good look at the other side of the Seine. Their legacy is burning to the ground, reduced to rubble. The eight towers will be no more. All eight families who built the Bastille brick by brick now see it destroyed the same way. Their rule is over. No need for the Fleur-de-lis now. It has served its purpose. A new France will be born."

"So you won't be carrying some vendetta into future generations?"

"No. I will not. Besides, the only ones who carry those vendettas are scorned women and nothing will stop them. Not even the devil himself."

So that's it. Somehow these eight families were responsible for building the Bastille, that's why they each got their name carved into a tower (not to mention scrawled on Michel's garret wall). Geez, nothing like carrying on a long-term grudge... That prison was built in 1382. Talk about remembering insignificant dates in history. But maybe I should have paid more attention to this one. Whoever the Fleur-de-lis were, that's what was motivating them. Revenge for the building of the Bastille. And to think I get ticked when Aeden brings up something I did like four or five years ago...

By now Monsieur Chastain was being supported by Simeon and Michel, covered tightly with Lizette's cape, the only visible part of his body being his neck and head. I could see the wound that that crazy Margaux made when she stabbed him on the stairs, and in that instant, I knew who killed our great, great uncle Henri. *The only ones who carry those vendettas are scorned women and nothing will stop them.* Where had I heard something like that before...?

Chapter Fifty-Six: Aeden

Ryn grabbed my elbow and pulled me back to the edge of the river. I watched as Michel and Simeon started to carry Monsieur Chastain away from us. Lizette was already ahead of them. I'd never see Monsieur Chastain again. Or Michel for that matter. The two people who protected me without question. My lower lip started to tremble and I raced towards them. But I had no words. None they would understand, anyway. It didn't matter. I grabbed Michel by the arm and then reached for his hand, squeezing it as hard as I could. Then, I leaned over and placed a quick kiss on Monsieur Chastain's cheek. That's when I saw the cut, still fresh from Margaux's knife. An imprint I had seen before.

The cut. The design. And then the colors came again. This time they wouldn't stop. Blue, indigo, yellow and pink. The street in front of me seemed to swirl around and suddenly I was wet again. Soaking wet. Had Ryn pushed me back into the river?

The colors pulsated until they blended into black and white. A high-pitched siren shot through my head and I started to choke on the water. My lungs were filling up. I could feel something tightening around my upper arm but couldn't free myself from it. The vertigo was horrific. I tumbled, twisted and turned in all directions. I was underwater. I had to be. There was no way my body could move like this on dry land. Then, I felt something beneath my legs just as my back landed on a hard surface. Around me, the screams and shouts from the crowd continued. Had the blood bath reached the other side of the river?

The dizziness was starting to subside, enough for me to open my eyes. And my hearing became more acute. Those weren't sounds of a manic, frenzied mob in the midst of a revolution. They were sounds of laughter. Shrieks, shouts and gales of laughter. My eyelids stuck for just a second as I pried them open. I was sitting on my rear end, drenched in the water from the Louvre fountain, just next to the pyramid. And Ryn was right beside me.

In front of us, an audience of spectators stopped to laugh as they made their way to the museum entrance. Ryn looked ever the part of a river rat and I started to laugh, too.

"It's not funny, Aeden. We're soaking wet and every part of my body hurts!"

"Your body? I'm lucky to be in one piece. I jumped off a tower for heaven's sake! A tower!"

"Well who told you to go climbing there in the first place?"

"But we did it, Ryn. We're here. That means we saved Monsieur Chastain and our ancestors, right?"

"Although we didn't stop Uncle Henri from getting killed."

"I know, but I have an idea who did it."

"If it has to do with the wound on Monsieur Chastain's neck, then I may have the same idea, too."

Just as Ryn and I started to stand up and step out of the water, someone was pushing their way through the line of people. I heard the voice before she even reached the fountain. Then, my mother starting screaming at us. I just prayed no one was putting this on You Tube.

"Ryn and Aeden! This is unbelievable! What are you two doing in that fountain? Horsing around, that's what! You can't even be trusted to enter a museum without making a spectacle of yourselves!"

Then, just as my father started to yell, the mother of that toddler who pushed us into time came rushing over, speaking as fast as she could in French and English.

"*Mon Dieu, Mon Dieu,* it is all my fault. My son just got away from me; running...and that boy and girl lost their balance and fell into the fountain. I am so sorry. *Pardonnez-moi.* I will pay for the cleaning of their clothes..."

"It's all right," my father said. "These things happen. No worries."

The lady smiled, picked up her toddler and walked off, just as my father lit into us like a brushfire.

"Do you have any idea who those two gentlemen are, standing off to the side? Well, I'll tell you who! They're from Interpol. Interpol! And do you know why? Because Ryn's French teacher was so worried about his safety, so concerned that he would be the next murder victim, that she contacted the International Criminal Police Organization! What on earth did you tell her, Ryn?"

Then before he could answer, my mother started in.

"I told you not to say anything to anyone. With Interpol here, the local police have no recourse but to share the information with the public and that will create a panic. They think there's a serial killer on the loose. That's why we came back to the Louvre, so you wouldn't get caught up in any publicity."

I cleared my throat, looked at my brother and spoke. And boy did it feel good to use the English language!

"We don't think it's a serial killer, Mom. Not a Fleur-de-lis anyway. And if Ryn and I could just have a little time in Uncle Henri's apartment, we may be able to find the real murderer."

Chapter Fifty-Seven:
Ryn

I've seen my parents pissed before, but this time my father was fuming. He didn't say a word during the entire ride back to the hotel except to apologize to the driver for getting the seats wet. I was glad it was Aeden who told them what we thought about the murder, because she stood a fighting chance of getting her way. All I would get would be an indefinite grounding. I kept quiet.

The ride to the hotel gave us time to decompress. That's the only word I can use to describe it. It wasn't like we were suffering through jet-lag, but something more unsettling. Like a total sensory hallucination combined with a script from some long movie or play. And if Aeden hadn't experienced the exact same thing as I did, then I'd really question my sanity. Great, great Auntie Zanne knew how to use prisms and light for time travel, so why didn't that crazy old lady have the common decency to write a manual!

I could tell that Aeden was still thinking about Monsieur Chastain and Michel. She had that sad, dreamy look she only gets when she listens to stupid songs or when someone sends her video clips of kittens. I left her alone. The brain fog I was feeling would only clear up with time.

It wasn't until the next morning that we were allowed to go back to Uncle Henri's apartment, but my parents insisted that I email Mademoiselle Claudine at the school first, in order to let her know that I might have been exaggerating and that everything was okay.

The room still looked the same and still reeked of old citrus. Aeden and I were allowed to poke around the living room as long as we "don't touch anything." How were we supposed to look for the clues we needed? That's like telling a hunting dog, "Point, but don't move." We moved. When my parents left the living room and sat down in the kitchen with the officer who escorted us here, Aeden and I started to piece together the few facts we had, beginning with what Michel said about the Fleur-de-lis. I reiterated it for her.

"He said that 'there was no longer the need for revenge; the revolution took care of that.' So...it couldn't possibly be some descendant who wanted to carry out an old vendetta."

"I agree," she nodded. "After going through all the trouble of saving us, Michel wouldn't expect future generations to murder our family members. That's why it couldn't be a serial killer. But who does that leave? Descendants of those guys in the cells that we wouldn't let out?"

"No, it was much more personal. I'll tell you who—a woman. A crazy, jilted woman. Uncle Henri must have walked out on some woman. Michel made some comment about scorned women being the only people who wouldn't let things go, and you know what's weird? I think I heard something like that before."

"Of course you did, you moron! It's an excerpt from a play that I was in last year. Of course, a very, very abridged version, but it came from 'The Mourning Bride' by William Congreve and he wrote it long before the French Revolution. So Michel must have heard that quote, too. Don't you remember me rehearsing those lines?"

"Aeden, I try really hard not to listen to anything you rehearse."

She stuck her tongue out at me but I kept on talking.

"You saw how nuts that Margaux lady was—trying to kill Monsieur Chastain. I bet there's a nutsy coo-coo woman in Uncle Henri's life, too, and just like Margaux, whose letter "M" appeared on the cloth napkin and on Monsieur's neck, this lady's initial had to be an "M" as well, because when it's written in cursive, it kind of looks like the Fleur-de-lis."

"Oh my God! That's where I saw the 'M' the first time, before I held that cloth napkin. The letter was painted on the top of that little Limoges box. We thought it was a Fleur-de-lis but it's not. It's someone's fancy initial. Hurry up, let's open it!"

Next thing I know, Aeden is staring at the little flower-shaped clip that unlocks the box.

"Well, are you going to open it or are you going to make three wishes?"

"Hilarious, Ryn, I'm just being careful."

Then, she slowly unlatched the small porcelain figurine and looked inside. I could tell by the sure, smug look on her face that we had solved the murder.

Chapter Fifty-Eight: Aeden

"Ryn and Aeden, if you keep procrastinating, we're going to miss the plane!"

My father had seen to it that all the luggage was already in the limo but my brother and I were both making sure we hadn't left anything behind. I paused as I glanced into Ryn's room.

"I really wish we had more time for sightseeing. And we never got to Versailles."

"That's how it goes, Aeden. Maybe next time."

"I don't think there'll be a next time. We only go places when someone dies."

"Yeah, I know what you mean. Dead relative vacationing!"

"But it turned out we were right all along, Ryn. It was a jilted lover thing. How awful! And just think, if we hadn't slipped back in time, we never would have seen the letter on the cloth napkin or witnessed first-hand how crazed someone could get. The woman who killed Uncle Henri was just as mad as that Margaux lady. What a coincidence that she had the same initial, too."

"Yep, Maurelle Dubriel. The little note she wrote inside the box gave it away. I guess old Uncle Henri strung her along for years and she couldn't take it anymore. And when her finances started to run out, she resented him even more. But she knew what she was doing when she slashed his throat. Sure, it was the letter 'M,' but she wanted it to look like a Fleur-de-lis to throw the police off. As an art curator, she knew a lot about history, so it was easy for her to pick the only thing that would make everyone go berserk—the resurgence of France's most infamous throat slitting society. And it almost worked, too, if it wasn't for that Louvre pyramid."

"I don't want to do it again, Ryn. You don't know how awful it was to be in a country where you didn't understand a single word anyone said and you couldn't reveal who you were."

"Oh, boo-hoo, Aeden, it's not like it was a picnic for me, either, trying to figure out what you were saying when you did use French. Ratatouille? Really? It's a vegetable dish!"

"I told you I knew foods..."

"You thought it meant mouse-rat!"

I rolled my eyes and started for the door. Then, I paused for one more thought.

"Promise me we're not going to use this knowledge to go gallivanting in any old place in time. I mean it, Ryn."

"I can promise...but promises get broken."

Chapter Fifty-Nine: Ryn

"Hurry up, Ryn. They've just announced our flight and Mom and Dad are waiting by the gate."

I was standing inside a little snack kiosk connected to a string of fast-food places in the Amsterdam terminal. We had to catch our connecting plane to Portland and the thought of airline food was revolting. Three chocolate bars, some yogurt raisins and a bag of pretzels were going to be my meal. Aeden could fend for herself.

"Okay. Okay, sure you don't want anything?"

"I'm sure."

"The heck you are, Aeden. You'll want one of my candy bars the minute we get on the plane. Hold on, I'm buying more."

As I turned back to the counter, I could hear someone yelling at us.

"Mademoiselle! Monsieur!"

It was the twenty-something guy who was sitting next to us on the flight over. He was still wearing those dark glasses and it looked as if he hadn't shaved in a day or two. But as he got closer, I couldn't believe who I was looking at. Aeden must've had the same reaction because she got very still and almost started shaking.

The guy reached into his pocket and pulled out a red scrunchy as he looked directly at my sister.

"I believe you left this on the plane when you first arrived."

I watched as she took the hairband from him, her eyes riveted to his hand.

"Your fingers are all black and blue. What happened?"

Then, he removed his dark glasses, lifting them slightly so they rested on the top of his head.

"Let's just say someone grabbed them a little too tight and...."

But before he could finish, there was an announcement for another flight. He smiled at Aeden and quickly walked away.

"Don't go slashing anyone's throat, Mademoiselle. No need anymore."

I started to run after him but they made the third and final call for our flight. Aeden and I raced to the gate and didn't say a word until we were seated. Then, she turned towards me and whispered.

"Oh my God, Ryn, did you see his face? It can't be. And you know what the weirdest thing was, he got off the first flight before we did. Then how did he get my scrunchy?"

"Face it, Aeden; maybe we're not the only people who know how to use prisms."

Then a taped recording of the plane's safety features ended our conversation. I un-wrapped a chocolate bar and handed her a piece. She was right about one thing. We only go places when someone dies. Geez, that better not happen any time soon.

Epilogue:
Monsieur Chastain

Supported by Simeon and Michel, Monsieur Julien Chastain staggered to the carriage. Exhausted by the ordeal and suffering from a minor concussion, he dozed in and out of consciousness as the driver wove his way through treacherous streets, still ripe with turmoil.

Simeon, Lizette, Michel and the Chastain housekeeper took turns caring for the master of the household. By nightfall, they no longer had to worry about the bloodthirsty mobs in the Paris streets. They had reached a small inn on their way to the village of Alençon in Normandy, where the extended Chastain family had lived and worked for decades, overseeing a bourgeoning lace industry. Renaud and Anjenet were already there with relatives.

Julien Chastain woke from his stupor asking for his children.

"Renaud, Anjenet, I need to see them."

"They have gone ahead, Monsieur Chastain," the housekeeper replied, *"and they will be safe. You need to rest for a little while before we can continue our journey."*

Three days and nights of unpaved roads, village inns and wayfarer rests blended into a seamless, timeless state as Julien Chastain struggled to regain his full awareness. By the time they arrived at the Chastain Chateau in Alençon, he was once again the man who had fled the Bastille with his children, taking every risk to ensure for their lives. But the boy and girl who greeted him had no knowledge of the events that had ensued.

"It must have been a strange dream, or perhaps an illusion, father," Renaud said as he looked closely into Julien Chastain's eyes.

Then, Michel spoke.

"The mind does strange things to protect the body. In your case, sir, it brought your children to you to help you flee the Bastille. A part of you must have known that you were no longer safe in that fortress."

"But it was so real, I could breathe the perfume on Anjenet's neck, I could see the dimple on Renaud's cheek."

"There are some things we will never understand and some things that we were never meant to."

The Chastains remained in Alençon and Michel became a trusted family friend. Although Julien thought he would never re-marry, he found himself betrothed to Charlotte Cloutier, the daughter of a wealthy industrialist. She gave birth to a son, Jean Michel Chastain.

The Chastain name was never crossed out from the list on the garret wall.

THE END

Endnotes

Timeframe and Events

This is a work of fiction and as such, I took certain liberties with the time frame and events that occurred on July 14, 1789. So, for the record, please note the following:

Historians concur that it was 3:30 p.m. on the afternoon of July 14, 1789, when the Bastille was stormed by angry citizens who had reached their breaking point with the government. The Bastille at that time held few prisoners, not hundreds, as works of fiction, including my own, may have implied.

The Bastille did anticipate an attack and had been preparing for it with guns and ammunition. But they never expected the huge mob that broke into the fortress. Ultimately, their governor surrendered and the flashpoint for the French Revolution began. The following sites will provide you with more information about this pivotal event in world history.

www.bastille-day.com/history
www.kwintessential.co.uk/articles/france/french-revolution-storming-the-bastille

www.thinkquest.org (Go to Library and Search for Bastille)

Please note: The Fleur-de-lis secret society never existed. Like the novel, it was fictional.

Image of the Bastille on the following page, "The Bastille View from the Southeast," copyright 2005, is re-printed with permission from Jim Chevallier.

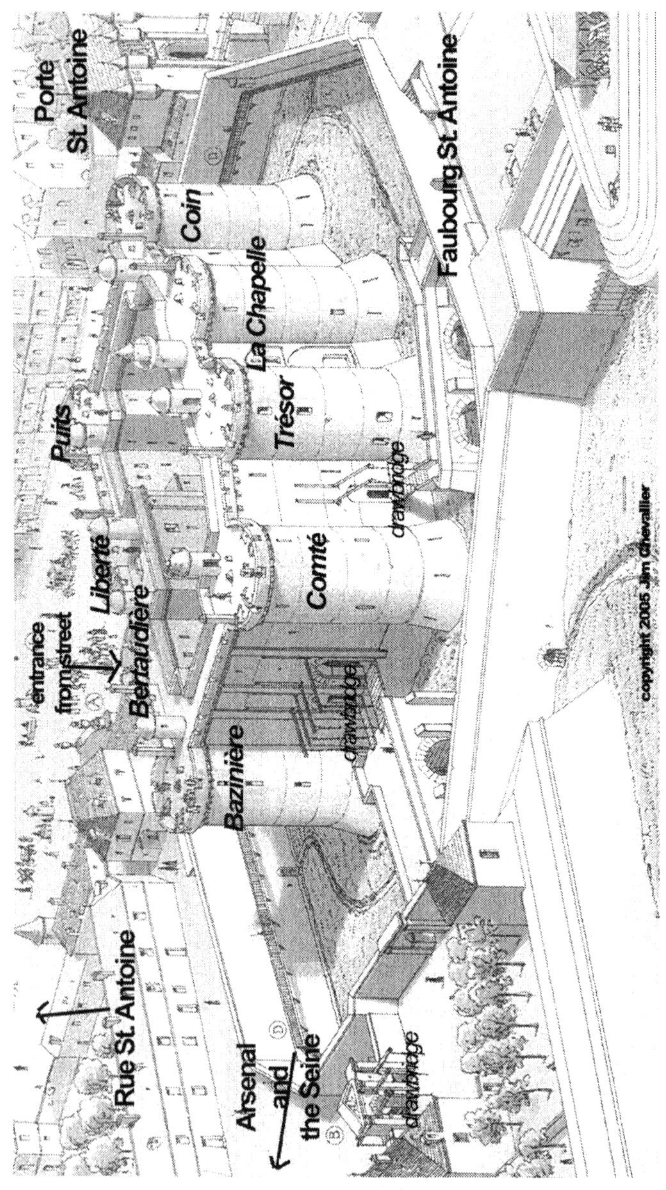
Porte St Antoine
Coin
La Chapelle
Puits
Trésor
Faubourg St Antoine
drawbridge
Liberté
Comté
entrance from street
Bertaudière
Bazinière
drawbridge
Rue St Antoine
Arsenal and the Seine
drawbridge
copyright 2005 Jim Chevallier

The Towers

In this work of fiction, the eight towers of the Bastille were named for those aristocratic families who allegedly financed the building of that prison. In reality, the Bastille was built during the reign of Charles V (1370 – 1383) as a military citadel and the towers were not named for French families. They were:

Basiniere Tower – Tour de la Basinière
Bertaudiere Tower – Tour de la Bertaudière
Chapel Tower – Tour de la Chapelle
Corner Tower – Tour du Coin
County Tower – Tour de la Comté
Liberty Tower – Tour de la Liberté
Treasury Tower – Tour de la Trésor
Well Tower – Tour du Puits

For further information about the towers, please visit: **www.decscubriparis.com**

Works Cited

www.discover France.net

www.emersonkent.com/history_dictionary/bastille.htm

www.mholyoke.edu

www.placesinFrance.com/history-bastille-paris.html

www.ruavista.com

www.skyscraptercity.com

www.thehistoryblog.com/archives/8693

Study Guide for *Light Riders and the Fleur-de-lis Murder*

This young adult adventure novel blends historical and science fiction. The study guide component provides teachers with differentiated questions and activities designed to develop thinking skills and promote a better understanding of this particular era in time. The study guide is reproducible for classroom use.

Chapters One–Five

1. Why does Ryn's attitude change about missing lacrosse practice?
2. Do you agree with Ryn's decision to study French?
3. Why do you suppose Aeden and Ryn's parents don't want anyone to know about the murder?
4. What kinds of things does Aeden do to annoy her brother? Have you ever done anything to annoy one of your siblings?
5. What makes Aeden's nightmare so frightening? What do you think will happen next?

6. Should Ryn have told Aeden the truth about what the passenger next to them really said? Explain.
7. What do you think the French word *arrondissment* means?
8. Why are the police so concerned about this particular murder?

Chapters Six–Ten

1. How does Ryn convince Aeden to go back in time? Write your own argument to convince her.
2. Ryn seems to have a knack of getting his way. Do you know anyone like that? What do they do?
3. If you were Aeden, would you go back in time with Ryn? Explain.
4. What happens as Ryn tries to use his French when speaking with the two police officers?
5. Draw a diagram of Uncle Henri's apartment. Be sure to label things.
6. What are the laws of refraction? * If you don't know, find your science teacher!
7. Aeden has a premonition that "something doesn't feel right." Should she be concerned? Explain.

8. What do you think traveling through time would feel like? Compare it to Aeden's description.
9. Where do Aeden and Ryn wind up, once they've traveled back into time? Should they be worried?

Chapters Eleven–Fifteen

1. List five–seven adjectives describing the place where Aeden and Ryn arrived, once they went back in time.
2. What year (or decade) do you think this is? Explain.
3. Aeden and Ryn follow an unknown man. Would you have done the same thing in similar circumstances?
4. What is the Bastille? What significance does it have?
5. Can you think of any modern day secret societies?
6. Why do you suppose some of the names on the wall in Michel's garret (room) were crossed out?
7. Draw a picture of Michel's garret. What do you expect to see?
8. Why do Aeden and Ryn go with Michel when they know he is about to kill someone?

9. Why does Ryn tell Michel and Alain that he (Ryn) will kill the Chastains?

Chapters Sixteen–Twenty

1. Michel and Alain, along with the others in their secret society, wish to change France by killing the aristocrats. Do you think murder is necessary for change? Give examples from history to justify your reasoning.
2. What are catacombs? Would you be scared if you had to walk through them at night?
3. Using internet research, find at least three images of catacombs and note the cities and countries where they were located.
4. Why do you suppose the dead were placed in catacombs?
5. Should Ryn have let Aeden return to the 21st century when she saw the people in the tunnel? Why or why not?
6. Do you believe time travel is just a force of nature that we do not understand? Explain.
7. Ryn describes two different Aedens. Is he overreacting or is she really the way he describes her? If so, why?

8. Yes or no. Ryn and Aeden are clever thinkers. Justify and explain using examples from chapters one–twenty.

Chapters Twenty-one–Twenty-five

1. How were French streets marked in the 18th century?
2. Why do you suppose Ryn and Aeden pretend to be Renaud and Anjenet?
3. Draw a picture of Anjenet's room, or, using your imagination, draw a picture of what you think Renaud's room would look like.
4. How do you think Lizette knew that Aeden was not Anjenet?
5. Find an old map of Paris and trace the route from the Rue Da Guerre to the Bastille.
6. Who wrote *A Tale of Two Cities?* * If you've never read that novel, put it on your reading list now!
7. Describe the atmosphere in the streets of Paris as Ryn and Aeden (aka Renaud and Anjenet) travel by carriage to the Bastille.
8. What is the significance of the date "LUNDI, JULLIET 13, 1789?"

9. Why does Ryn refuse to acknowledge Michel when he sees the man at the Bastille?
10. Compare Monsieur Chastain's room in the Bastille to the filthy dungeon that Ryn expected to see.
11. ***advanced question:** Why did people throw straw down on the streets in Paris?
12. ***advanced question:** How did the accommodations at the Bastille differ?

Chapters Twenty-six–Thirty

1. Aeden says that the Bastille "engulfed her like a giant accordion." Can you re-write this simile using a different comparison?
2. Why do you think Aeden grabbed the ring of keys and ran out of the room?
3. Why do you suppose the woman from the kitchen helps the Chastains?
4. What plan does Ryn have?
5. Do you think there is significance to the names on the wall? Explain.
6. Would you have opened the cell and let Edouard Favreau escape? Why or why not?

7. Should Ryn really have been that concerned about how he smelled? What would you be like under the same circumstances?
8. How would you describe the way Aeden is handling the situation, considering the fact that she does not understand French?

Chapters Thirty-one–Thirty-five

1. How do you know that Ryn is really unnerved about having to remove a dagger from a dead person? Could you have done the same thing under the circumstances?
2. What are cognates? If you don't know, find a foreign language teacher!
3. Yes or no. Ryn understands his sister's capabilities. Use examples to justify your response.
4. Pretend you are Ryn. Write two- four sentences convincing Michel to help the Chastains get out of the Bastille safely.
5. Have you ever used the argument "You said so yourself." Explain.
6. Does Ryn trust Michel? Do you?
7. What is a garderobe?

8. Yes or no. Monsieur Chastain genuinely cares about his children. Use examples from the text to justify your answer.

Chapters Thirty-six–Forty

1. Would you have jumped the moat like Ryn or climbed the wall like Aeden?
2. Draw a sketch of the embedded stairwell. Why is it dangerous?
3. If you were Aeden, what would you have done if a little mouse crawled up your sleeve?
4. Why did the Chastains and Michel need to spend the night at the Bastille?
5. What will happen at 3:30 p.m. the following day? (July 14, 1789)
6. How did Aeden know that a woman had occupied the room?
7. Who is Margaux and what do you suppose happened to her?
8. Should Ryn and Aeden have opened the cell door in order to give food to the unknown prisoner? Justify your reasoning.
9. Why would Lizette want to protect Aeden?

Chapters Forty-one–Forty-five

1. Ryn crisscrosses a ceiling on a narrow plank to help his sister. Have you ever taken a risk to help someone? Explain.
2. Why did the woman on the stairwell try to kill Monsieur Chastain?
3. Describe what you think it would be like to slide on a sewage chute under a river.
4. What do you suppose Michel meant when he said, *"Au Revoir Artois?"*
5. Draw a picture of the scene in the river.

Chapters Forty-six–Fifty

1. Who is trying to kill Aeden and why?
2. Should Aeden have stayed in the river? Could she have stayed? Explain.
3. According to Ryn, "What always happens in horror movies?" How did it happen here?
4. Why couldn't Aeden turn around and go back to the river?
5. What do you think is going to happen next?
6. What does Aeden mean when she says, "My God, what have I done?"
7. What scares the living daylights out of Ryn? What do you think he should do?

8. Did Aeden make the right choice to climb the tower? What other choices, if any, could she have made? Explain.
9. Yes or no. Michel is a hero.

Chapters Fifty-one–Fifty-five

1. Ryn decides that the only way to escape with their lives is to start a massive explosion. Do you agree? Explain.
2. Were there ever times in history where extreme measures were taken in order to save lives? Give examples.
3. Can you solve the puzzle of the eight aristocrats and the eight towers?
4. * If you read *Light Riders and the Morenci Mine Murder,* who does Ryn refer to when he ignites the fuse for the first keg?
5. Should Monsieur Chastain have killed Margaux when he had the chance to do so in the river?
6. Why is Aeden no longer angry with her brother? Do you think her attitude will change later on?
7. What was the significance of the white flag?
8. Do you believe Michel when he says that there is no longer a vendetta? Explain.

Chapters Fifty-six–Fifty-nine

1. Where had Aeden seen the same imprint as the scar on Monsieur Chastain's neck?
2. Upon returning to the 21st century, where are Ryn and Aeden and why is everyone laughing?
3. Why is Ryn's father so furious with him? Does Ryn's father have a right to be so angry? Explain.
4. How do Aeden and Ryn solve Uncle Henri's murder?
5. What does Ryn mean when he says that his family only does "dead relative vacationing?" Do you think this is the case for other families? Why?
6. Is the guy from the plane really Michel? Justify and support your answer.

Epilogue

1. How does Michel explain the strange events to Monsieur Chastain?
2. Why do you suppose Michel remained with the Chastain family? Would you have done the same thing?

If you could travel back to any era in time, where would you go and why?

Thematic Classroom Projects:

- Compare the timelines for the American and French Revolutions (history)
- Compare the motivations for the American and French Revolution (history)
- Create a scale drawing of the Bastille (art, architecture, history)
- Study the Laws of Refraction (science)
- Learn about actual secret societies in history (history, psychology)
- Motivation for revenge (social sciences)

Acknowledgments

I owe a tremendous amount of gratitude to my editors who continue to probe, push, and persuade so that the quality and substance of my writing continues to grow. And of course, to my proofreaders who manage to catch the most minuscule details that ultimately make all the difference.

USA – Ellen Lynes, Susan Morrow, Suzanne Scher, Steve Somers, Lisa Tonks

Australia – Susan Schwartz

Special thanks to my technical support team for their research, expertise and advice.

USA – James Clapp, Beth Cornell, Larry Finkelstein, Gêne Stickles

Author Jim Chevallier (www.chezjim.com) was kind enough to let me re-print his image of the Bastille and I am indeed grateful.

ABOUT THE AUTHOR

New York native Ann I. Goldfarb spent most of her life in education, first as a classroom teacher and later as a middle school principal and professional staff developer. Writing has always been an integral part of her world. Her freelance non-fiction can be found in trade magazines for Madavor Media and Jones Publications, but her real passion is writing mystery-suspense for young adult audiences. Time travel is the vehicle she has chosen to embrace.

Ann resides with her family near the foothills of the White Tank Mountains in Arizona.